ILLUMINUS

The Induction

Nedra Brown

Illuminus: The Induction

Copyright © 2022 by Nedra Brown

To contact the author, email nedrab25@gmail.com.

ZYIA CONSULTING
Illuminate & Transcend

Zyia Consulting
Book Writing & Publishing Company
www.nyishaddavis.com
nyisha.d.davis@gmail.com

ISBN: 9798986116617

Cover Design: Dev Designs / dev.designs@yahoo.com

Printed in the United States of America.

Dedication

I dedicate this book to Dr. Lawrence Rogers Burwell for being a great example and reminder of what Black Excellence looks like. Thank you for sharing your stories with me.

Acknowledgment

I would like to acknowledge Dr. Roger Lawrence Burwell for being a daily reminder and inspiration to me. Thank you, Dr. Burwell, for reminding me that there are no obstacles that can't be faced head on when approaching your dreams. Lastly, thank you to Nyisha D. Davis for opening a window of opportunity for me to create, publish, and build on my aspirations as a writer and creator.

TABLE OF CONTENT

1

The Distressed

Elizabeth Smith was an average young woman going about her daily life like all the rest of us. She spent most of her days working. After establishing herself as a young entrepreneur, she was determined to make ends meet. Her Virginia nights consisted of dreaming of all the possibilities that awaited her as she tried to make her way through college. Elizabeth studied during the night and made her way through her online courses that consisted of loads of work that didn't seem to be manageable in the way she would have

preferred. She struggled to finish grad school as she siphoned through what little savings she had left from the money she was allotted.

Each day was the same. She woke up to her anti-social cat, Sprinkles, who didn't seem to care for her company at all. Elizabeth prepared for her stressful job as a financial assistant to wealthy financial advisors for the infamous World & Trust Bank. Elizabeth hated her job. It was stressful at times, pretentious, and the minority population consisted of her and only her. She hated getting up daily, waltzing her way into a building where the population was predominantly white, ostentatious and competitive.

She entered the building, and left behind all true emotions, as she plastered on a fake smile and dished out fake compliments and laughter to her co-workers she could not relate to. What was it that kept her planted in this bubble of unhappiness? Why was it that when she looked around the room there was no one who looked like her? These were questions she asked herself daily.

Elizabeth tried to overlook the obvious feelings of inadequacy. She clung to the hope that one day, a new hire would walk through the door with her same complexion and complexities for life. But that was not the case, nor would it ever be.

Elizabeth planted herself at her desk, and kicked off her stiletto pumps. She thought to herself how today felt more like a chunky heel kind of day, due to the throbbing within the arch of her feet's deep tissue. She turned her phone volume down, placed her blazer on the back of her chair, and planted herself in the necessary mental space she needed to get through the day she felt certain would be a rough one; like all the other days she had been experiencing in her new work environment.

The door of her office swung open unexpectedly. She looked up in annoyance and realigned the look on her face as she took notice of her most unfavorable coworker, Katherine. "Well then, good morning to you, too," Katherine said as she stood in the doorway dressed in an all-black banana republic pantsuit, with her cleavage bursting at the seams. She looked as though she had selected a shirt that was two sizes too small for the rack that was currently greeting the entire office before she could.

"Good morning," Elizabeth said as she looked away. She wanted to appear as if she was currently engaging in work that was keeping her eyes busy as well as her mind. She was hoping to steer away from the unwanted co-worker's attempts to engage. "What can I do for you?" Elizabeth asked as she watched Katherine make her way around the office. She looked at every corner, touching things as if she was currently a detective in the middle of an investigation. "I just stopped by to see how you were adjusting to the new office," she replied. Katherine looked as if she could care less as she spread her treachery meticulously through the air.

"It's a nice office," Elizabeth responded, waiting for Katherine to get to the point. She felt as though Katherine wanted more than to see how she was "adjusting" to her new space. "Well, I also wanted to know if you had gotten a chance to look at the Bronson account. Maddox said he felt like someone should give you a little reminder because it looked as though maybe you were falling behind."

There it is, Elizabeth thought to herself as she tried to suppress her frustration while she pictured herself slamming the office door in the face of the nosey blonde who didn't seem to mind protruding in the affairs of others for sport. "I was told that Maddox would be handling the Bronson's account," Elizabeth replied. She felt confused as to why someone would assume that was an account she would be responsible for after being told the account belonged to someone else.

"Well, I'm not sure," Katherine said as she shriveled up her face with disapproval walking away. She knew what she had accomplished after seeing how bothered and disheveled Elizabeth had become after her pessimistic attempt to derail her. Katherine exited the room, leaving Elizabeth to stew in a pool of worry and confusion.

Once again, she had been misled and couldn't help but to wonder if her co-worker, Maddox, had given her the wrong instructions purposely. After all, how could he make such a huge mistake telling her the account belonged to someone else?

Elizabeth stared at the clock. It read 8:30 a.m. She felt a surge of frustration explode on the inside as she tried to process and plan out her day. She had craved for placement into the field of financial advisement for so long. Yet, it did not feel like the kind of environment she had envisioned. She thought about the life she had left behind in New York. What was it that kept her from doing what it was she needed to do to be happy? She did not know.

Elizabeth had left behind New York City's fast-paced environment, a stagnated unhealthy relationship, and a trail of unsuccessful career attempts to move back to her hometown of Richmond, Virginia; all to try and obtain a more sensible and less chaotic way of life. She heavily relied on the support and guidance of her childhood best friend, Johnathan Meadows.

Johnathan was about 5'8" with dark brown skin, and a warm and reliable personality. Johnathan and Elizabeth had been best friends since the third grade. They both experienced numerous major milestones with the other by their side, as best friends should.

Elizabeth picked up her phone. She began to construct a text thread. She was anxious to cry out to the only person in the world she felt cared enough about her issues in life to sit and actively listen. She began texting expeditiously, implementing every stressful detail about what had taken place with Katherine. She conveyed to Johnathan how she was certain her co-workers were plotting to destroy her peace. Her phone rang instantly after submitting the text. She answered and felt instant relief as soon as she heard Jonathan's voice on the other end.

"What's going on now?" He asked while already feeling certain that Elizabeth was having another one of her emotional outbursts after being taunted by her co-workers. "I can't do this anymore," she replied. She attempted to hold back the tears that were currently festering up in both eyelids. Her emotional overtones of distress began to pile up in the back of her throat.

"Tell me what happened," Johnathan said as he prepared himself for a long, drowned-out description of Elizabeth's daunting morning. "They don't want me here. I am starting to realize that, and I feel like I don't belong. Katherine came into my office this morning claiming to have wanted to check in to see how I was doing. She began raiding around, touching my things, acting as if she was embarking on an innocent journey of girl-on-girl support. She asked me about my progress on an account that I was originally told belonged to someone else."

Elizabeth started to let the tears flow freely as she told Jonathan about her innermost thoughts and emotional responses to event after event, leading Jonathan to finally interject. "Let me ask you something," He said in a stern tone, making Elizabeth aware that he was ready to lay down the foundation to a more interpersonal chat concerning her job and the emotional turmoil it was causing her. "How do you feel when you walk into your job?" He heard the long pause in Elizabeth's tears ending as she pondered on the question. "I feel...

I feel…I don't know."

She tried to avoid the question and replied in a frustrated tone. "I think you're lying," Jonathan said firmly. "I think you do know how you feel. So, I'm going to ask you again. How do you feel when you walk into your job?" He waited patiently for a more truthful response. "I feel miserable," she replied under her breath, in a way that conveyed to her close friend and unappointed therapist that she was ready to break down the walls of denial and let her truth reign freely. "I feel like I'm forcing myself to do something I don't really want to do. When I analyze my life path, being a financial assistant makes sense, based on the imagery. But, other than that, I have no real reasoning for why I continue to try to do this."

Johnathan sat silently on the other end taking it all in. "What do you mean by imagery?" "I just feel like this is one of those jobs that looks good on paper, or sounds good when you open your mouth to tell people who you are and what you do. But, other than that, there's nothing that feels fulfilling outside of those components. I feel like I'm sabotaging myself internally for a career I have zero passion for," Elizabeth continued.

Jonathan spoke up, breaking his silence after Elizabeth had finally revealed what he had already known to be true. "How can you expect to be happy in a position that brings you no internal fulfillment?" He waited for her response. Elizabeth sat silently for an elongated portion of time, thinking about Johnathan's question. The words 'fulfillment' and 'happiness' rang in her mind loudly as she tried to make sense of her choices that clearly were not the best. "I can't," she said in an emphasized tone. Once again Jonathan had unintentionally helped

Elizabeth to see the real root of her issues.

"I know what I need to do," she said as she thanked Jonathan again, and dismissed herself from the call that had given her the introspective paradigm she had been unable to see prior to Jonathan's phone conversation. Elizabeth gathered her emotions and exited her office quickly before she could be spotted by anyone. She feared the look on her co-workers' faces if they caught her walking around the office with mascara smudges present on her face.

She glanced in the mirror for minutes, before she removed the makeup from her face. She assessed the bags under her eyes that could only be properly hidden with a small trace of concealer. Who was this woman staring back at her? She thought to herself as she analyzed the transition she had made in a short period of time. Stripping her of everything she knew of herself internally.

She began to wish for the presence of her mother who had been deceased for the past six months. Elizabeth couldn't help but feel as though things had gotten worse after her mother's passing. She gazed at herself again, and looked deep into herself. Elizabeth wondered what the purpose of this new journey filled with adversity was all about. She searched for the strong driven young lady she had always been, and looked for the young woman who had been full of fire and determination. But, that image was not the image staring back at her. Instead, she saw the reflection of a tired young woman, torn, and losing her ability to fight for the things she had envisioned.

She began applying the finishing touches of concealer under her eyes, finishing powder to her face, and her favorite Lancôme lipstick to complete her look. She reentered her office with a more normalized appearance, leaving behind the mascara smudges and unsettled energy that had plagued her at the beginning of her morning.

Elizabeth sat at her desk and began pulling up the Bronson's account. She assessed what she could do to get the account up to par. Katherine and Maddox could keep infringing upon her peace all they wanted. But, that would not keep Elizabeth from prevailing. Sure, she had shed a few unnecessary tears and held up Jonathan's morning with her emotional outburst. However, giving up was not something she was accustomed to. She picked up the phone and attempted to reach out to Mr. Bronson immediately.

Katherine may have had her fun prying at Elizabeth, but she had no clue who she was dealing with. Elizabeth pressed on with her day determined to prove herself in a short period of time. Her mother had always taught her that there was beauty in being the underdog. If they weren't going to allow her to pull up a chair and have a seat at the table, then she was going to take a seat against their wishes.

Jonathan sat at his desk, and glanced at the photo of him and Elizabeth. He thought about his innermost feelings and all the things he loved about her. The feelings he had managed to keep hidden since childhood. There were so many, how could he just pick one? The two of them had been friends for so long, and made their way through life relying on one another. Their bond consistently evolved and they grew closer and closer as the years carried on.

Jonathan thought about what Elizabeth had to be feeling at the current moment. It had been weeks now that she had spent the majority of her days contacting him infringing upon his workday. She told him about countless taunting encounters with her unwelcoming gang of co-workers. He had always known Elizabeth to be a fighter and was not used to the girl he would nowadays deem to be fragile and easily moved. Jonathan knew Elizabeth was having a hard time and felt it was due to the passing of her mother. This is what kept him being her listening ear. Even in times where he had prior dedications of his own to attend to.

His phone rang, interrupting his thoughts. "Hello," Jonathan said. "Mr. Meadows, your eleven o'clock has arrived," Taylor said. "Thank you, Taylor. Send him in," Jonathan replied.

Omari Bronson was a professional football player who had earned himself a successful fortune, after becoming an athlete turned entrepreneur. Omari's career erupted, shooting him to the spotlight abruptly in 2015. For it was shortly after his rise to fame and fortune that he started seeking out the help of his now long-term and reliable therapist Jonathan meadows.

Omari sat in his usual spot on the brown and moderately worn out sofa while he waited for Jonathan to initiate the start of their session. "How are you doing today?" Jonathan asked as he glanced up at Omari. He took notice of his awkward disposition. "I'm doing ok," Omari replied, looking as if he was anything but ok. "Would you prefer we pick up where we left off last week or would you like to start somewhere fresh?" Jonathan questioned while still assessing Omari's body language. "I'm not sure," Omari replied, sending out one distressed image after another. Jonathan began scanning through his notes from his last session with Omari. He searched to find a reasonable starting point.

"When we last spoke, you were discussing how you felt overwhelmed. You expressed feelings of inadequacy in relation to your career and success. Why don't we start there, and you can explain to me what it is that makes you feel this way."

Omari began to express his thoughts. "My entire life I dreamed of becoming a ballplayer. I started out playing little league football. Then, I went on to play in high school and eventually college. Every game I played hard, giving it my all, dreaming that one day there would be someone watching in the audience waiting to offer me an opportunity of a lifetime. This was my dream, and probably every other person's dream that played on my team."

"My dad and my mom made it to every game since I was a kid. They never missed out on an opportunity to see me shut it down on the field. One day, I was approached by a scout during my first year of college. He approached me asking if I would be interested in coming to play for a professional team in the NFL. I didn't think twice."

Omari took a long pause in his story, appearing to be battling with the idea of whether he should continue. "What happened next?" Jonathan asked to keep the story progressing. "After the game, I met with the scout and we set up an official meeting the following week. The week arrived for the meeting and my parents and I were going to meet with the scout. But, the morning we were to meet with the scout, I received a phone call early that day urging me to come alone. I was so excited I didn't think it mattered that they didn't want anyone else there. I explained to my parents that they wanted me to come alone. I remember them both looking at me crazy, telling me that something just didn't feel right. My mom kept telling me to keep my guard up, but I didn't listen."

"That morning, I remember arriving at the address, looking at the rose park residence in awe. I felt like I had walked into a dream come true. When I arrived at the five-story home, there were two men dressed in all black suits who appeared to be security waiting outside in front of the entrance."

Omari took another long pause, preparing himself as he readily began to confess something he knew could potentially have him killed. He froze up, making himself mute for a more elongated portion of time. "Are you ok?" Jonathan asked as he observed the fear and withdrawal in Omari's eyes. He took another pause appearing to want to flee away from his story once again. Omari's hands started to tremble as he sat on the sofa, preparing to take a much-needed stance in the right direction after all the trauma and pain he had experienced.

"We can stop here if you'd like and pick up again next week," Jonathan suggested. "I'm ok," Omari responded. "I can continue. I need to continue," he said in a distressed tone. "As you wish," Jonathan said as he jotted notes in his notebook about Omari's physical demeanor.

"Where was I?" Omari asked. He had lost sight of which portion of the story he was currently engaged in telling. "You walked up to the entrance where the security guards were. Then what happened?" Jonathan asked. "I entered the house and was approached by a third guard. He took my phone, patted me down, and then led me up a staircase to an office where I was seated in front of an empty desk. I sat and waited for the arrival of someone else. However, no one ever showed up. Ten minutes later, a loud voice pierced through the speakers that were mounted to the wall. A woman started speaking to me. She asked me how I would feel about the opportunity to have everything I desired." "Under what pretenses?" Jonathan asked, sensing the story was taking an unusual turn. "She asked me what I would be willing to sacrifice for a membership into the Illuminus Society." Jonathan glanced up, "The Illuminus Society?" Omari looked back at Jonathan with an odd look on his face. "Yes, the Illuminus Society."

"The Illuminus Society is a large secret society that is funded and founded by an African-American for other African-Americans. It is a society that was founded in the early days by African-Americans who were looking to build themselves, and their lifestyles after the fall of the culture of the slave and indentured servant. The rumor was said that early members included people like Madam C. J. Wallace, Malcom Luther King, James Washington Carver and The Tempters."

Jonathan looked up at Omari after hearing the names of the individuals and resonating with The Tempters, having grown up in a household where his grandparents and parents played music from the infamous group on a notable basis. He was starting to become consciously intrigued with the direction Omari's story was going. Jonathan repositioned himself in his chair. He tried his best not to appear anxious on the outside as he prepared himself for the continuation. "I heard rumors while being inside the organization that Malcom Luther King was approached and asked to be a member of Illuminus Society. But, he was assassinated the day before his scheduled induction," Omari continued. Jonathan looked up again, feeling even more intrigued by the foundational background information of the secret society he had never known existed.

"I don't want to interrupt, but I would like to ask you something," Jonathan said. Omari glanced over at Jonathan as he prepared himself for the question. "Sure," he replied. "What is the purpose of this alleged Illuminus Society?" Jonathan asked out of mere intrigue. Omari took a long pause fearing his explanation would sound preposterous. "The society was created to help influence the projection of black excellence. The society wanted to help motivate those who had lost their confidence and purpose after being a part of the slave culture. Black people had grown tired and needed something to believe in. So, a freed slave named Samuel Lincoln Brown started the organized society."

"This society sounds interesting," Jonathan said, glancing over at Omari. He wanted to make sense of his distressed facial expressions as he listened to him continue with his story. "Everything isn't what it seems to be," Omari replied. "The society continued to grow after being established on January 31, 1870. Samuel started recruiting local black farmers, aspiring inventors, and local creatives who had dreams that were far bigger than the forty acres and a mule they never received. Before you knew it, word started to spread far and wide and within a few years, Samuel Brown had organized a full-fledged secret society that contributed to the growth of the black culture and lifestyle. As the story goes, the members started to see a rise in success, gaining more income to build business, own property, and reestablish lifestyles that were far more plentiful than the ones they had originally known," Omari concluded.

Jonathan felt more and more intrigued by Omari's story as he got further into the details. It sparked a few questions in Jonathan's mind. Just as Jonathan began to part his lips to ask his question the timer chimed alerting them that they had reached the end of their session. "I'm afraid that's all the time we have for today. We will pick up again on Thursday," Jonathan said as he held onto his questions while making a mental note to jot them down.

Omari agreed, thanking Jonathan quickly as he made his exit from the office. Omari felt instant relief. He had broken down the walls of anxiety he had mentally constructed within himself when he thought about coming clean and professing his induction into the life-changing society. What had once felt like the opportunity of a lifetime was now beginning to unravel into a never-ending nightmare. He didn't know how much time he had left. He felt the clock ticking daily as he made his way closer and closer to freeing himself by voicing his truth. Omari knew telling Jonathan all he knew would not be his ticket onto redemption road, but it was definitely a start. He hopped into his 2020 Tesla, replaying his therapy session in his mind.

He started the vehicle, preparing to head home when his phone started to vibrate. The caller identification read, "Unknown caller." Omari debated if he should answer. The phone vibrated again. He picked it up uninterested in who it might be. "How are things going?"

The voice asked. The voice caused Omari to feel startled as he recognized the female tone on the other end.

Omari took a long pause before attempting to respond. "Things are good," he said as he anticipated the purpose of the call. "I am going to be recruiting new members soon. I need to know I can count on you to help," the voice inquired. Omari sat silently again not uttering a word as he debated on the proper response. "Can I count on you?" The voice asked again. "Yes, yes, you can count on me," Omari replied. As he took in the sound of the dial tone that rang abruptly in his ear.

2

Indiscretions

Could she count on him, she wondered as she sat at her desk. She quietly thought about the feeling of uncertainty that was currently plaguing her as she tried to find solace. But, she could not. She had been at the forefront of all components of Illuminus for over 100 years now. And each day was starting to feel longer than the others. What was it about his tone that didn't sit right with her? Was he having second thoughts?

She had recruited Omari into the Illuminus Society five years ago. Ever since his inclusion, he had seen nothing but abundance. Surely, he could not betray her now. Not after all the paid endorsement deals, luxury, and most importantly a spot on one of the top teams in the NFL. He was indebted to her. And if he wasn't, there would be dire consequences.

Just as she tried to think about what she should do about her feelings of concern regarding Omari, her office door opened. "I'm sorry, Queen Mother. I don't mean to intrude," Magnus stated with a nervousness present in his voice. "May I come in?" He asked. He kept his feet glued to the floor just in case she declined. "What is it, Magnus?" She asked, looking to be uninterested in his unscheduled visit.

"I have the list of potential recruits you requested," he said. Magnus waited for her to invite him in as he spoke to her through the small opening of the door that was slightly ajar giving him just enough of a visual to assess her mood. "You may enter," she said as she showed no interest in the timid recruit who was shaking in his boots at the sight of her presence.

"Who do you have for me?" She asked. Queen Mother hoped this year's list would be more phenomenal than the previous five. Especially after her thoughts of distrust that was now starting to surface about Omari. "I have a significantly larger list to pick from this year," Magnus said as he laid out pictures of each recruit onto the table.

Magnus sorted the pictures into two piles. One pile with the male recruits, and the other with the female recruits. She glared over at Magnus as he stood silently still holding the same timid demeanor he had entered the room with. "Got damit, Magnus. Don't just stand there. Give me the rundown!" she yelled aggressively. "Yes...yes... Queen Mother," he stammered with a stutter present in his voice.

Magnus was five feet tall, with a noticeably hunched back and a cocked eye. He suffered from Kyphosis ever since infancy, due to a malformation of his spinal bones that appeared to have worsened over time. Magnus had spent his entire life feeling the sharp dagger of pain and trauma invade his being. He had a face that only a mother could love. Every day of his life was a reminder of that until he was recruited into the Illuminus Society.

His father was a drunken drifter who stumbled into a small-town diner located in the heart of Mississippi where he was originally from. He swept Magnus's mother off her feet, moved in, and came and went freely never truly establishing himself as a partner, provider or father. Magnus's mother never looked at him in a way that made him feel inferior like everyone else around him. She showered Magnus with love, care, and fairy tale stories, hoping to make him feel as though there was a place for him somewhere in the cold world he had not been welcomed into with love and promise like most infants.

Madeline screamed and screamed as her contractions began to get closer and closer. Jack, or Blackjack as everyone liked to call him, was nowhere in sight. Madeline had been rushed to the hospital in her neighbor's small two-door vehicle with no one there to comfort her. They reached the hospital, and she was admitted into labor and delivery. The doctor rushed into the room, assuring Madeline that it was now time to deliver her baby.

Madeline screamed, "He will be here! Just wait! I know he will!" She yelled while the tears flooded down the sides of her face. He would not and she knew he wouldn't. "Ma'am, we can't wait any longer. We have to deliver him now," the doctor said. Madeline knew she could not wait. The contractions were getting stronger, and her pain was now becoming unbearable. Once again, Jack had let her down. While she lay in a hospital room pushing through her contractions and delivering their child, Jack sat at a nearby bar drinking his miserable existence away until he was too drunk to form a complete sentence.

Madeline screeched out in pain as she gave her last and final push. Out came her baby, crying loudly overwhelming the entire room. Madeline looked up as she noticed the silence from the health care team. "What's wrong?" She asked. The nurse handed the baby over to the head physician immediately, shielding her from having a clear visual of her baby.

Madeline had lost an excessive amount of blood and her blood pressure began to drop tremendously. "Is there something wrong with my baby?" She asked as she began to drift in and out of consciousness. The medical team escorted the baby out of the room while they began to do a blood transfusion on Madeline right away.

Jack came staggering into the hospital, after receiving Madeline's voicemail, barely able to stand upright. "How can I help you?" The receptionist asked as she looked at him with a judgmental expression plastered on her face. "Madeline, Madeline Leary. I'm here to see Madeline Leary. She is having my boy," he said while falling over, using the receptionist desk as an aid to help him hold his drunken position.

"She's in room 202. But, it appears she has just been taken into surgery," the receptionist said. "Surgery? What kind of surgery?" Jack asked, filling the air with the aroma of whiskey and cigarettes. The receptionist frowned her face up after getting a whiff of his whiskey -stained breath. "It appears she experienced some complications after giving birth, and will not be able to have visitors right now," the receptionist said as she assessed the constant stumbles as Jack appeared to become aggressive with her.

"I need to see my woman and my baby!" He yelled while banging on the top of the desk. "Sir, I'm afraid that won't be possible," the receptionist repeated. "Listen here," Jack said while slightly staggering over the top of the desk with no coordination in any of his moves or hand gestures. "You're gonna let me back there. And you're gonna let me back there now! Or else I'm gonna, I'm gonna," he said before collapsing completely to the ground.

The guard that was standing adjacent to the desk rushed over to help Jack up off of the floor. "Baby are you okay?" A voice called from the background. A little petite woman with tight curls began approaching the receptionist's desk. The receptionist frowned her face up instantly as she took notice of what was occurring.

The petite woman bent over attempting to help Jack up off of the floor, managing to irritate him instantly. "Get off of me woman!" He yelled in a rageful tone. "I can do it myself," he said as his words continued to slur from the whiskey that had now become completely settled in his digestive tract.

"Sir, you're gonna have to leave," the guard said after feeling annoyed with the drunken charade that had gone on for quite some time, causing the receptionist to feel extremely uncomfortable.

"I'm sorry, baby. I was just trying to help," the petite woman said as she took notice of how aggressively uncoordinated Jack had become since his departure from her vehicle. "I told you to stay in the damn car," he said as he picked his ego up off the floor. He realized he had made a complete fool of himself. The two exited the hospital and left the lobby dwellers to converse about what they had witnessed.

"Yvonne, I told you to keep your ass in the car," Jack said to project his anger onto her after realizing he had exposed and completely embarrassed himself. "Well, Jack, if I hadn't gotten out when I did who knows what would have happened back there." She tried to speak up for herself, and explain why she left the car after being instructed by Jack not to leave the vehicle.

Jack had been seeing Yvonne during the same duration of time he had been enthralled in a relationship with Madeline. Yvonne knew of Madeline's existence, but Madeline knew nothing of hers.

Yvonne drove the car in silence as she tried to drown out Jack's drunken snores that were overwhelming her ability to think. They had driven over an hour to get to the hospital for Jack to see the birth of his son only to have him show up drunk and embarrass himself. Yvonne couldn't help but feel low on the inside as she assessed herself as a woman. Here she was riding around with a drunk loser in the front seat of her vehicle whose favorite pastime was bar engagements, mismanaging money and juggling women. Surely this was the curse her grandmother spoke of when she repetitively yelled at her as a young girl; "You will never be anything more than a man stealing floozy." Surely her grandmother couldn't have had any true inclination of who Yvonne would become.

But, it was her alarming outer beauty that created a noticeable divide amongst her and the women in her family. Every family dinner, church meeting, or gathering Yvonne would have to overlook the inappropriate stares of the men who were attached to her aunts, the negative glares from the women who despised her for her beauty, and the quiet whispers of how she would be just like her mother.

Yvonne's mother was also a very beautiful woman who had very little resources in the small community due to her beautiful face, and her heartless desire to lay down with any man she took interest in no matter if he was single or not. This behavior made Yvonne's mother, Shirley, greatly despised amongst the community. Especially with the married woman who often feared when it would be their turn to lose their man to Shirley's tactful, yet, very tacky intimate engagements with the elite and married male population. Yvonne was the spawn of a very infamous local married preacher who had engaged in an extensive extramarital affair with Shirley and gotten her pregnant.

When Yvonne was born, the pastor and his wife left town, leaving behind the trails of gossip, dysfunction, and the visual reminder of Shirley's beautiful baby girl left in the mind and heart of both the pastor and his wife. Although they had fled and left behind the pastor's indiscretion, Yvonne was left to pay for the sins of her mother and father. Their actions led her to live a life that lacked self-love, self-worth, many times a lack of self-awareness, along with the many curses that had been verbally spewed out at her as a child who knew the familiar imprint of verbal abuse dished out to her from her caregivers.

After the pastor's departure, Shirley left Yvonne behind to live with her grandmother, Mama Pearl. Rumors spread throughout the small town that Shirley had left to become a madam running a brothel for other beautiful husbands stealing floozies just like her, according to the women in the town. But, Yvonne never believed that.

Yvonne felt ugly on the inside. This was something she often felt due to her abusive background. But, today was not like all the other days of feeling a lack of self-worth. She thought about Madeline Leary, laying in a hospital bed after having complications due to childbirth.

Madeline was a beautiful woman just like Yvonne. However, Yvonne had always felt like Madeline was the better woman. Madeline was smart, kind, and educated. She spent her days teaching as a math teacher and her nights waiting up for Jack to return home to distribute his half-ass rendition of love that she often accepted. She looked past his outer exterior. Madeline felt for the weak man who preferred drowning his feelings in a bottle of whiskey every night to escape the truths that tormented him daily. Both, Madeline and Yvonne, shared this character trait in regard to how they handled Jack's shortcomings in the relationship.

Yvonne tried to place herself in Madeline's shoes. How would she feel if she had been laying in the hospital, giving birth to a child alone with her partner running around town, drinking himself into a slumber, and parading around with another woman? Yvonne had thought of this scenario many times before, each time feeling the guilt of what she was doing. But, she always allowed selfishness to take over as she made herself believe that she somehow needed and deserved Jack. After all, who else was there?

Tears began to fall from her eyes as she glanced at herself in the rearview mirror. All she saw was a pretty face with an empty needy soul. She needed so much from Jack and none of it appeared to be things she was actually receiving. Was this desire real? Or was it just her way of making herself believe it was real so she could continue to engage in a relationship she knew was wrong? She hated thinking of all the times she had been compared to her mother as a kid. But, today was a day she was starting to feel that maybe there had been some truth to those comparisons.

She pulled up to the front of her house, and noticed Jack was beginning to wake up. She started thinking of tactics that could potentially get him to stay. Nonetheless, she knew he would not. There wasn't a hot meal or massage in the universe that would keep him from running back to Madeline and she knew it.

Yvonne couldn't help but feel disappointed with herself. Once again, she was lowering herself for a man she knew would never solely belong to her and only her. There was something about having someone that felt better than having no one at all. She knew her only option besides leaving Blackjack alone would be to walk away and restore her dignity. She knew dignity was not going to keep her warm at night.

So, she did what most women in her position would do. She stayed. She stayed silent. She stayed unhappy. And she stayed ashamed at the hurt she was intentionally causing another woman out of pure selfishness and low self-esteem. An indiscretion is an indiscretion. But, how could something so horrible provide so much solace for another? She thought to herself as she exited the car gracefully, preparing yet again to watch the man she had formed an unhealthy attachment to walk away to go be with another woman.

She had heard stories for years about her mother's indiscretions. She was a product of indiscretion. So, why couldn't she break the cycle, walk away from her own indiscretions, and be okay with the gloomy period of loneliness while she waited for her next relationship to present itself? This was a question she could never be bold or honest enough to answer. So, for now, she would continue to dabble in her indiscretions for it was the one place of comfort she knew. That was something she and her mother had in common.

Yvonne prepared the table for dinner. She tried not to make eye contact with Jack who appeared to be coming out of his drunken slumber. "Baby, I made your favorite," she said in a soft tone, praying he would not decline one last sit down before rushing off to Madeline's side. "I ain't staying," he said. Yvonne looked up at him, acting surprised. "So, you're gonna let me eat alone?" She asked. "I have to get back up to the hospital and check on my family," he said in a stern cold tone.

Yvonne's ears rang with aggression every time she heard Jack utter the phrase "my family." She feared this would be the dynamics of their relationship forever. She realized that she would always just be Yvonne to him, and they'd always remain his family.

She watched Jack exit without so much as a goodbye. He often got like that after his alcohol levels dropped because it was then that he was able to fully assess himself and get a clear visual of who he was and who he should be. Yvonne watched the door shut behind him as she sat at the table in front of the meal for two.

She had been enjoying Jack's company so consistently, she had somehow convinced herself that he would be staying with her permanently when she knew he would not be. She stared at the hot meal while it rested on the plates with the hot steam floating into the atmosphere. She could no longer eat. Her appetite had evaporated into thin air as she thought about Jack nestled up in the hospital bed with Madeline and their perfect little baby.

Yvonne stood up in a rage. She began tossing the plates from the table and throwing them to the floor. She picked up the side dishes and tossed each one after another, hearing the glass shatter until there was nothing left to throw. Once again, she was faced with the hard truth that her indiscretion was causing her more hurt than help. How many more times did Jack need to run to Madeline for her to understand that she was never going to be the only one?

Yvonne's Grandmother Pearl had always told her to never pray to God for a man. Especially, if he has proven himself to be no good. But, that wasn't advice she wanted to take into account when thinking about how the birth of the baby was going to change the dynamics of their relationship.

Yvonne fell to her knees out of desperation. Sure she had been taught that it was wrong to pray to God for a man, especially if the man belonged to someone else. But, she did not know what else to do. She closed her eyes and said a silent prayer, asking God to remove Madeline and the baby from the picture so she could have Jack all to herself. She finished her prayer, as she fell to the floor. Yvonne balled herself up into a fetal position and cried and cried. She felt worthless and pathetic. After all, who prays for a man with a newborn? She asked herself silently.

Madeline lay in her hospital bed still feeling weak after her blood transfusion. The doctor walked into the room to check on her, and give her an update on the baby. "How are you feeling, Miss Leary?" The doctor asked. "I feel fine," she replied, leaving out her true physical feelings in hopes to see her baby soon. "I know you're probably eager to see your baby. But, I wanted to speak with you before we brought him into the room." Madeline sat up in the bed. She prepared herself for what she had assessed from the look on the doctor's face, bad news.

"It appears your baby boy was born with Kyphosis. A severe curve in the spine and has a few abnormalities," the doctor said in a soft tone. "Due to the curve of the spine and some issues with the tissue located near the bone, we cannot perform surgery to correct it because it could kill him," he concluded. Madeline didn't shed a tear while listening to the doctor. For in her mind she felt blessed just to know her baby boy had survived.

"Can I hold him?" She asked, interrupting the informative style conversation she was not interested in having. "Sure, you can. But, first I wanted to know if you had any questions or concerns before we bring him in." "No, I don't,'" Madeline replied as she lay anxiously in her bed waiting for the nurse to retrieve her baby boy.

The nurse entered the room, holding the baby boy with the malformation. She handed him over to Madeline. The nurse feared how Madeline would respond after taking a look at him. Madeline held the baby boy in her arms, and began to sob quietly. She looked at his soft brown skin and his bright eyes. She could feel the malformation of his spinal column protruding through the blanket wrapped around him, but she did not mind. Madeline did not see the cocked eye, or the curved spine when she looked at her baby. Instead, she saw a beautiful blessing she knew she needed to love and cherish no matter what the rest of the world would feel towards him.

Madeline looked into her baby's eyes, feeling in awe of the bright eyes that were glaring directly back at her. "I'm going to name you Magnus, in commemoration of your big bright eyes that magnify in the light," she said softly to the baby as she observed him. Magnus looked back at her as if he understood what she was saying to him. Madeline continued smiling, and talking to her baby.

Suddenly she smelled a recognizable stench, floating through the air. She looked up to find Jack standing in the middle of the room. He smelled like an opened bottle of whiskey. "What is that?" Jack asked, assessing the physical abnormalities that could be noticed from a mile away. Madeline looked at him and did not answer. "What the hell is that?" Jack asked again to pull an answer out of Madeline as he tried to make sense of their baby's physical appearance which did not match the baby he had envisioned for nine months.

"This is our son," Madeline said firmly in a soft tone. She tried to refrain from alarming the baby she was becoming attached to by the minute. "That damn thing isn't my baby," Jack said as he exited the hospital room quickly. He showed Madeline who he truly was, a coward. Madeline didn't shed a tear or utter a word to Jack as he made his exit.

If he couldn't accept Magnus and look past his abnormalities, she did not want him around despite her feelings of love for him. She made a vow to Magnus, at that moment, to never be with or around anyone who wouldn't see him in the same magnitude as she did. It would be a promise she would keep until her dying day.

Yvonne picked up the last of the glass particles. As she continued to clean up her mess, she got herself in order physically and mentally. She noticed headlights flashing in her driveway. She instantly felt anxiety come over her body. She tried to assume who it could be. She was concerned because she had been contacted consecutively for weeks by an organization claiming to have the ability to give her all of her heart's desires if she became a member. But, she had not given in to their invitation. Were they some kind of cult worshipers who had felt disrespected by her decline in their offer and had now come to harm her?

As she thought of all the worst-case scenarios her mind could wrestle up, the door swung open. In came Jack, walking back through the door. "What happened in here?" He asked as he took notice of the leftover mess Yvonne had not been able to dispose of. "I had an accident," she replied, leaving out the details of her deliberate destruction of dinner due to his departure.

"I thought you were going to the hospital to check on Madeline and the baby," Yvonne said while secretly jumping up and down inside at the sight of his arrival so soon. "I did," he said in a bland tone. "You did?" Yvonne repeated, feeling confused as to why he had returned so soon. She looked over at him as he sat silently on the sofa. He did not say anything in response to her inquiry

"Well, what happened?" She asked again to get him to give her something. "The boy isn't mine," he said in a low tone. He acted candidly as if it were of no real significance. "What do you mean he isn't yours?" Yvonne asked. "It ain't mine and that's all you need to know!" Jack yelled to bully Yvonne into asking fewer questions. "I'm sorry," she said softly, as she put a lid on her questionnaire, and joined him on the sofa.

Could this be real? She questioned silently. Sure, Grandma Pearl had always told her that it was inappropriate to pray to God for a man. But, had God somehow taken pity on her desperate soul, and given her what she had just prayed for? Or, was she getting ahead of herself? Surely, the answers would not come to her overnight. But, for now, she was just going to be grateful, that for another night, she had Jack all to herself again. Indiscretion or not, he was hers for the night, and she would deal with the sting of his departure once that time came again.

3

Changes

Magnus continued to spread the remaining pictures across the table. He categorized a total of thirty potential recruits. "Go on, give me the rundown," Queen Mother restated this time in a much more inviting tone. She tried to encourage Magnus to feel less anxious. He glanced up at her slightly, preparing to start with the most promising candidates first.

"First, we have Irene Holmes from Canada. Irene is a twenty-five-year-old scientist and published author. She recently published a book where she reestablished some major scientific claims. She is a bestselling author of a book where she focused on breaking down Einstein's theory of relativity. Holmes introduced new information with well supported evidence to Einstein's Quantum Theory earning her a lot of attention. The twenty-five-year-old scientist has had sit-downs with CNN, The Today Show, and Oprah to name a few," Magnus concluded.

"Next we have Jessica Braxton. Jessica is a college student and violinist. Braxton was a late bloomer and didn't start playing the violin until her third year in high school. Once she started playing, she quickly learned how to read music and became first chair. She held the number one spot while being pinned against musicians who had been playing the instrument since the age of four."

"What does this Jessica study?" Queen Mother asked. "Jessica studies anthropology and music at NYU. Her current G.P.A. is a 4.0 and has been since her initial entry into the university. What makes Jessica quite interesting is it appears she is studying biological anthropology. However, she appears to have an elevated knowledge of all four fields of anthropology, deeming her an overall candidate of black excellence," Magnus continued as he watched Queen Mother grow bored with his description of the potential candidates.

"Wow me, Magnus," Queen Mother said. Magnus started assessing the categories. He tried to target the best potential 'wow' candidate. He reorganized the candidates. This time he categorized them from most to least excellent, and reproached his description with a new set of front runners he felt Queen Mother would approve of.

"Next, I have agent Karen Black. Black is a twenty-seven year old retired FBI agent," Magnus said as he gave a slight smirk. He anticipated Queen Mother's intrigue as to how a black woman could or would retire from the FBI at the age of twenty-seven. "Why so young?" Queen mother asked, inquiring about Black's early retirement. "Black entered the FBI at the age of eighteen getting accepted as a special agent..."

"Will I have to wait until Christmas?" Queen Mother asked in an impatient tone. "Or can you speed this up, and get to the part about what makes Black so exceptional." "Sure Queennnn Mo...Mother,"

Magnus said with a stammer reemerging in his dialect. "No reason to get nervous, Magnus. You're doing great," Queen Mother assured him. She hoped he would calm himself and continue at a faster pace. "I apologize for my rudeness, Magnus. I'm just feeling a little overwhelmed, and I need this year's recruits to be exceptional," she continued. "The…the…they will be," he stammered on.

"You may continue," she said, nodding her head, signaling him to go on with the description of agent Black. She waited patiently for the wow factor to pop up somewhere in his description "During her ten years as an agent, Black closed over thirty cases, fifteen of which were cold cases, and shut down three major crime rings in New York," Magnus continued as he noticed the spark in Queen Mother's eyes. This spark was the spark of intrigue and investment. Agent Black sounded like the kind of woman Queen Mother took high interest in.

Magnus continued, "Black left the FBI after experiencing a traumatic loss. She had been working to bring down the Ramona crime family and became compromised. The Romano's learned who Black truly was. They kidnapped and killed her brother along with his two daughters who had recently lost their mother to cancer six months prior to the kidnapping. Black blamed herself and decided to leave the FBI. She fell off the grid completely shortly after her departure."

Under normal circumstances, Queen Mother or any other listening party would have asked at that very moment how such a thing could be possible. How could Black possibly be found if she had indeed fallen off the grid for such an extensive period of time? But, she knew better than to ask such a stupid question.

Magnus was many things. In fact, some would argue that looking at him stripped away a person's ability to believe that there was more to him than his alarming physical appearance that left most assuming he had no worth whatsoever. But that was not the case. Magnus could track down anyone in the world. No matter how significant or insignificant they could appear to be in the grand scheme of things. He used his combination of wit, elevated intelligence, and tech-savvy capabilities to track down the untraceable in as little as seventy-two hours. This was a quality that had proven to be a very useful one amongst the members and potential members of the Illuminus Society. For it was Magnus's talents that assisted the Queen Mother in locating those she felt could help continue to build the legacy Samuel had left behind.

"Where do you think this Agent Black is located?" Queen mother asked, having an idea of what her motive could be for suddenly deciding to fall off the face of the earth. "I've been doing some digging, and so far there are no clues as to where she may have gone. But my guess is she is somewhere tracking down the people responsible for the death of her family," Magnus stated, as he assessed the intrigue in Queen Mother's eyes.

Judging from the look on her face, it appeared to him that Karen Black was just the kind of badass she loved to come by. Queen Mother was an unusual woman, who held more power than any man she had ever come into contact with. There was something about a strong fearless woman that made her smile.

She knew that if there was anyone who could track Black down, it was Magnus. Magnus continued going through the list of potential candidates when he was cut off. "No need to continue. I'm sure you'll make me proud," she said as she signaled for him to exit the room to continue his work. As he exited the room, Queen Mother pondered around the idea of what to do about her concerns in regard to Omari.

Magnus made his exit prepared to track Black down as soon as possible. He came upon a huge bookshelf that was filled with books. The shelf was covered in popular literature. Magnus reached for a specific title. The title he selected was "Roots" by Alex Haley. He grabbed the book and pulled it towards him without properly lifting it off the shelf. The bookshelf began to roar loudly as it turned slowly acting as a hidden door.

Magnus walked into the entryway behind the shelf. He made his way down the hidden staircase as he heard the bookshelf close behind him. Magnus walked into a room covered in huge screens, video monitoring devices, and computer technology that appeared to be more advanced than the average technology found in a home or office. Magnus used this technology to track down and surveil all of the inductees. This was how he kept eyes, ears, and a location on everyone to make his job doable.

He sat at a station that was covered in technologically advanced devices and began pulling up monitors and accessing cameras that appeared to be in different locations in the outside world. He pulled up screen one where he appeared to have a visual on Elizabeth Smith. She was currently being surveilled by the Illuminus Society for a potential induction opportunity.

He had been watching Elizabeth ever since the passing of her mother to get an idea of who she was and what her routines were so he could know when and where to approach her with an offer. Magnus switched his direction. He wanted to see who else was currently being monitored on one of his spy screens. Magnus glanced at one of the screens in surprise as he watched a woman exiting a retreat in Bali. Magnus clicked on the spy screen making the image of the woman bigger. It was just as he had expected. He had located Karen Black in less than twenty-four hours as he had intended. He hit the oversized red button located at his tech station setting off a silent alarm.

The alarm was connected to a room located on the second floor of the home. The silent alarm alerted the induction team instantly. It sent an elite squad of men, dressed in soldier-like attire, out of their room and to the front of the house. Magnus slipped on his jacket, grabbed his carry bag swiftly, and slipped an unusual looking laptop into his bag. He exited the hidden room and joined the soldiers as they all lined up, waiting for further instruction.

Captain Ivin Silver stepped forward as the leader of the Induction army, awaiting his instructions. "I have located a potential inductee. Retired FBI agent Karen Black." Magnus said as he assessed the magnitude of the team waiting in line for him to take the lead. "She is currently hiding out at a retreat located in Bali. We are to retrieve her and bring her here in one piece. Black is most likely armed and dangerous. She will not be an easy retrieval," Magnus warned. "So, let's do our best to be diligent and get her back here safely," He continued.

The group of soldiers gathered into the helicopters expeditiously ready for their first assignments after months of complete stillness amongst the Illuminus Society. Captain Silver gave his men further instructions of what to do to ensure a successful and safe capture of agent Black. The team departed on their journey to locate the exceptional agent to help Magnus welcome her with the invitation of a life-time.

Jonathan pulled up to the entryway of his home. He contemplated if he should go in or turn around and continue driving. While he sat in the car, he felt drained from a long day's work. Inside, he knew his fiancé awaited his arrival. She would be preparing a hot meal while she made wedding plans on the phone with her mother, without Jonathan's inclusion of how the day would go.

Jonathan had been dating Alicia Gibson for three and a half years and was suddenly experiencing a change of heart in relation to his feelings for her. Jonathan felt ashamed every time he looked at himself in the mirror. He had spent his entire life preparing for the new beginnings he was starting to walk into. But, somehow, he did not feel content in any of it.

Alicia was educated, smart, and reliable. Yet, there was a consistent urge tugging at him daily. Jonathan didn't know what to make of this confusing feeling he was currently struggling to tackle daily. There was nothing that Alicia could do that seemed to make the urge go away. She only influenced the feeling to retreat for a few short moments at a time, before it somehow found its way back into his mental space. It caused him to feel the internal sting of unhappiness as he played along.

Jonathan sat in the car deep in thought. He tried to figure out how it was that he got into the very same space he tried to help some of his clients get out of on a daily basis. He had never been one to live a lie. Nevertheless, day after day, he found it harder and harder to own up to his true feelings as he watched Alicia plan for a life, he had figured out he no longer wanted to be a part of.

Jonathan turned off his engine and forced himself to exit the car. He entered the home with the beautiful woman waiting to share wedding plans with him. "Good evening, Mr. Meadows," Alicia said pleasantly. Alicia glowed with wedding plans still present on her face. She juggled greeting her soon-to-be husband and babbling on the phone with her mother about the proper dress style for her big day. Jonathan tried to avoid conversation. He felt plagued by the thought of having to engage in a conversation about wedding cakes and proper attire for a day he knew would never come. He felt disgusted with himself, but not enough to open his mouth and tell Alicia the truth. So, instead, he did what any selfish egotistical man would do in his position and he continued to lie and play along.

Jonathan placed his coat and bag in his office. He then locked himself in the bathroom while he tried to drown out Alicia's wedding talk that was floating around in the background innocently. Jonathan glanced at himself in the mirror and tried to figure out who he was becoming. It had never been his normal nature to lead a woman on, but it was something about his situation that made him feel guilty, like telling Alicia the truth would do her more harm than good.

Alicia was loving, but fragile in a way that seemed equivalent to a child. Jonathan hated feeling like he was betraying her. However, he also didn't want to feel responsible for breaking her heart. Jonathan had come to the revelation of his true feelings for Alicia over six months ago, shortly after discovering he had feelings for Elizabeth. However, he couldn't stomach the pain of seeing Alicia disappointed in that way.

He gazed at himself a little longer to consider how Alicia would feel once she found out the truth. He wanted to storm into the living room, interrupt her conversation, and explain to her that he was no longer interested in getting married. But, he did not.

"Babe, dinner is almost ready!' Alicia yelled out to Jonathan. He did not respond. She called out to him again, but there was still no answer. Jonathan had become so enthralled in his feelings and thoughts of shame that he could not hear anything outside of his own intrusive guilty emotions. Alicia banged on the door to get his attention.

"Jonathan, are you ok in there?" She asked. "I'm okay," Jonathan replied, lying through his teeth. "Dinners ready," she said, sensing that something was not right. "I'll be out in a moment," Jonathan said as he began to prepare himself for another night of fake laughs and phony interaction as he yet again pretended to be in love with a woman he was no longer interested in.

Alicia set the table and sat in her chair silently while waiting for Jonathan to join her. Was he having cold feet? She questioned to herself. She tried to erase the thought from her mind by telling herself there was no possible way that could be the case. After all, Jonathan had spent months talking to her about starting a family and moving forward as an item. There was no way he could be having doubts.

Alicia brushed away the anxiety and resubmitted a smile as she watched Jonathan reenter the room. Jonathan sat at the table, appearing to be still somewhat distant. "Is everything okay?" Alicia asked while assessing the look on her partner's face. She had never seen Jonathan conduct himself in such a manner and she did not know what to make of it.

"Everything's fine. I just had a long day. One of my regulars came in for a session, and I can't help but wonder if I should have extended our session and let him continue," Jonathan replied. "Extend his session"? Alicia asked, instantly buying the story Jonathan was pitching to her about his awkward display. "I got the feeling he really needed to finish, or at least he wanted to, but I cut him at his normal time."

"Well, there's always next week," Alicia said not understanding what a difference in a few days would be. "I can't put my finger on it, but I got the feeling after he left that he needed to get the rest of his story out and in the open. There was something about his body language that came off really distressed," Jonathan said. "Well, why didn't you?" Alicia asked. "My morning started off rough, because I didn't get much sleep last night. Then Elizabeth called me with one of her morning meltdowns. I guess I was a little burnt out so ending the session seemed like the right thing to do."

Alicia rolled her eyes and became silent. She was suddenly no longer interested in the conversation. Jonathan knew what her issue was and felt it was best to retreat away from the conversation entirely. Jonathan sat at the table and consumed his dinner in silence. He watched Alicia's facial expressions go through an array of changes before she decided to speak her mind as he knew she would.

"I just think it's strange how often she calls you with her personal problems," Alicia said. "And why is that?" Jonathan responded, sensing the beginning of another one of Alicia's brushes with insecurity in regard to Elizabeth. Alicia made it no secret that she did not favor or agree with the relationship dynamic between Jonathan and Elizabeth. And if it were up to her, the relationship between the two would have ended a long time ago. However, she knew that would never happen. Jonathan had spent the majority of his childhood by Elizabeth's side. He made it clear to Alicia that he would never change that for anything or anyone.

"I just don't understand why it is always you she reaches out to for every little problem in her life." Alicia continued not hiding the jealousy in her tone one bit. "I mean what is she going to do when we get married?" Jonathan continued to ignore Alicia, fearing he would say the wrong thing. Especially after all the other feelings he currently had raging through him concerning the two women.

He sat at the table pretending to listen, shoveling his food from one side of the plate to the other. He prayed Alicia would soon stop talking. However, she did not. "I mean it's really quite pathetic if you ask me," Alicia continued. "But, I didn't," Jonathan said sternly, surprising Alicia with his remark. "Excuse me," Alicia said, "What did you say?" she asked. "I said I didn't. As in I didn't ask you," he said, looking at her in a way she did not recognize. "You are constantly taking jabs at Elizabeth; she's pathetic, she's needy, etc. But whether you like it or not Elizabeth is a part of my life, and she always will be. I've known her ever since we were kids and she's always had my back."

"I know she calls a lot and lately it's starting to look like I'm always helping her through something, but that's what friends do.

There was one point in time when the tables were turned and she was always there for me. So, now it's my turn to reciprocate that," Jonathan said. He left no room for a rebuttal from his jealous counterpart. "Keep in mind, Alicia, when you're judging Elizabeth she just lost her mother. Everyone doesn't have the luxury of a rich quantity of family and friends." Jonathan concluded, leaving Alicia to stew in her poor taste in judgmental commentary about his best friend.

Alicia sat quietly, and tried to come up with a new conversation in hopes to erase the tone that was currently floating through the air like the aggressive elephant in the room that should have not been touched. Jonathan was no longer in the mood for conversation. And, judging from the look on his face, he was not making it a secret.

Eventually, Jonathan apologized to Alicia, blaming it on a hard day at the office and a lack of sleep. He excused himself from the table while Alicia sat alone to assess and understand his sudden elevated aggression. Alicia sat at the table frozen in thought. Jonathan had never been that rude and aggressive. She couldn't help but notice all the changes he had displayed since his arrival home. Was it her? Was she not giving him what it was he needed to be happy? Alicia became flustered with anxiety instantly embarking on one self-assessment after another.

She tried to figure out if she had done something wrong to make Jonathan change in regard to his approach to her. Alicia couldn't help but wonder if there was more to Jonathan's relationship with Elizabeth than what he had initially told her. After all, he was soon to be walking down the aisle with her. Yet, she couldn't help but to notice that during their conversation Jonathan seemed more defensive and concerned about Elizabeth than her.

She picked up the phone and attempted to call her best friend, Tamra. She was ready to spill out all of her flawed perceptions of the night's events. But, there was no answer. Then the phone rang, interrupting Alicia's thought session. "Hello," she answered, feeling annoyed with the fact she had been questioning her future from a minute dinner squabble that was insufficient in size and quality.

"Well, it took you long enough," Tamra said, referring to the number of rings prior to Alicia answering. "I mean you called me first," Tamra said giggling on the other end, but there was no reciprocation of laughter. Instead, her moderate sense of humor was met with uncontrolled sobbing. "What's wrong?" Tamra asked. She got no reply. "I know my jokes aren't funny, but there's no need to cry." She continued to get Alicia to calm down and tell her what was going on. Alicia continued to cry.

Tamra waited and waited for the sobbing to diminish. However, Alicia kept going unable to reply to Tamra's inquiry. "Do I need to come over there?" Tamra asked as she mentally prepared herself to do so. "I can hop in my car and get there in fifteen minutes," she said while slipping on her furry slides and oversized cardigan preparing to do just that. Suddenly, there was a pause in Alicia's tears and she started sniffling and suppressed her loud cries for help.

"I...I...," she said, being interrupted by her sniffles as the tears continued to die down. "I think Jonathan is having second thoughts," she said. Alicia felt a sting in her heart as she openly said it out loud to her friend. "Girl, I know you didn't call me and get my blood pressure skyrocketing for this," Tamra said as she began to laugh out loud.

Tamra's reply alarmed Alicia as she tried to understand what was funny about her emotional outpour

"Tamra, I'm serious. I think Jonathan is getting cold feet and doesn't know how to tell me," Alicia said with an unusual sense of urgency and assurance present in her voice. Tamra paused, realizing she was serious. "Girl, I think you're just overanalyzing things. Jonathan loves you and he is a psychologist for goodness sake. The man makes a living helping other people learn to be okay with expressing their innermost thoughts and feelings. I don't think Dr. Feelings, himself, would be walking around hiding his own," Tamra assured her friend, as she heard Alicia's sniffles continue to suppress. Alicia began to take in what Tamra was saying. Alicia felt crazy. Tamra had made a very good point. Jonathan was the king of expression and open conversation about feelings and thoughts.

There was no way a man who had built his entire career around the art of communication would be reluctant to share his own feelings with his partner. "Girl, I think you just need to take a chill pill and calm your senses. Jonathan loves you. There's no way he'd be having cold feet because you're smart, funny, and have an annoyingly hideous laugh that only a genuinely tolerable person could put up with," Tamra said. She was able to get Alicia to dish out an earnest laugh. Alicia took in the compliments from her friend who had managed to alleviate her from her countless anxiously flooded thoughts about the future of her relationship.

"Where is all this coming from anyway?" Tamra asked. "I don't know," Alicia replied. "Lately, it just seems like Jonathan is off in outer space. I'm starting to notice the more I talk about wedding plans the less he does altogether." "Girl, he's a man. It's his natural nature to not care about the details. That's our department," Tamra said to get Alicia to see that she was overreacting.

"Yeah, I guess you're right. Maybe I am overanalyzing things. I guess I just envisioned this time with Jonathan to be going a little different," Alicia concluded, "I'm sure you did. Sis, I've told you that you watch too much T.V.," Tamra said, making fun of Alicia as she speculated the fairy tale visions Alicia pictured for her wedding plans and engagements.

"It was just something off about how he responded to me at dinner. Everything seemed fine. Well, maybe not all the way fine, because I sensed he was different. As soon as he heard me mention Elizabeth's name, he went flying off the hinges." Tamra interrupted, "Girl, here you go with this Elizabeth mess again. I knew I should've hung up on you when I heard the first set of tears. You need to get over your suspicions of him and Elizabeth and let that man have his friend, who is his childhood friend in peace. You wanting him to dispose of his friendship with this woman would be like him wanting you to get rid of me. It's unfair and insensitive to his history with her. So, if you are jealous, just say det!!!" Tamra said jokingly, getting Alicia to loosen up, realizing her feelings towards Elizabeth and Jonathan's relationship was ridiculous.

"All relationships experience changes. You just have to determine which changes you're willing to go through and to what magnitude," Tamra said. "You're right. Change is change and some change is good. Maybe I'm experiencing these emotions because it's me who needs to make some changes," Alicia concluded.

4

What Lace?

Giselle Howard ran swiftly through the alley. She picked up her pace with every step, as she reached for the pepper spray that lay in the bottom of her oversized handbag. She heard steps in the distance. The assailant sped up each time she attempted to do the same.

She was dressed in her usual flamboyant fashion-forward attire. This attire wasn't the most comfortable outfit selection when attempting to outrun a potential rapist or kidnapper, she thought to herself. She continued to power walk. Giselle was certain she could buy herself enough time to dig for the pepper spray and escape her approaching assailant.

The steps began to get closer and closer. This sparked a feeling of fear, as a lump began to form in her throat. She envisioned with trepidation how it was going to happen. She knew better than to be out late at night, walking the streets alone. Giselle's mother had always talked to her about the importance of being prepared for danger. Yet, somehow, she was not in the mood to face whatever evil entity was tailgating her in human form.

She needed to drop her bag and make a run for it. But, there was no way she was parting with her custom-made Louis Vuitton carry bag. She had spent a pretty penny on the bag and felt as though if she was going to be taken out the two would depart together.

Giselle had been working stressful hours all week and was starting to feel like she was losing what little marbles she had left. Sleep deprivation was something she struggled with significantly, and it often challenged her ability to see and think clearly.

She sped up and finally reached the front door of her cousin Tamra's apartment. Giselle could hear Tamra talking loud in her normal gossipy tone on the phone. Giving someone relationship advice as she overlooked her own relationship flaws. It had been three weeks since Giselle had seen or heard from her cousin. Giselle never felt the need to schedule a visit, being as though her pop-up visits were always welcomed.

Giselle ran to the door banging loudly, disrupting Tamra's phone conversation. She looked back over her shoulder periodically to see if anyone was lurking in the shadows. But there was not a soul in sight. Tamra opened the door in a rage. "Why the hell are you banging on the door like you're the police?" Tamra questioned as she took notice of Giselle's awkward demeanor. "What's wrong, Selle? She asked as Giselle came rushing in like she had been running away from someone or something. "Can I get something to drink?" Giselle asked as she sat on the leather sofa ready to pull herself together.

She panted frantically, as she glanced over at her alarmed cousin. Giselle tried to make an effort to catch her breath once more. "Sure, but what's going on?" Tamra asked, feeling disturbed by the look on Giselle's face that she could not make sense of. "I don't know what's going on with me," Giselle replied as she sat quietly still trying to make sense of the last few days.

"I don't know what's going on with me. I've been plagued by this weird feeling the past couple of days," she said. Tamra handed Giselle the water as she listened to Giselle talk in circles not seeming to make any sense to her at all.

"Maybe you're just tired, Selle. Besides, it's not normal to work so much, or so often without rest. And, you do that a lot. Like a damn zombie," Tamra continued as she watched Giselle gulp down the glass of water quickly without taking a pause. It was as if she had not drank anything the entire day.

"I'm sorry," Giselle said as she took notice of Tamra's facial expressions. "Earlier in the week, I had decided to go out and grab lunch with a friend. I had the oddest experience." "What do you mean?" Tamra asked. "I went out and I was impatiently waiting for an Uber. It was not long before I decided to walk. The entire day, I couldn't shake the feeling I was being watched or followed. I made it to the restaurant and noticed there was an unusual looking man who came in a little after I got there who appeared to be watching me." "Watching you? Watching you how?" Tamra asked in an alarming nature.

Giselle was a petite and extremely attractive young woman who spent a lot of her time roaming around the Richmond area on her own. It made sense to Tamra that a man would be interested in getting a look at her in a restaurant. What didn't make sense to Tamra was why

Giselle would be under the impression someone was following her.

Giselle had been working as an entrepreneur for the past two years, running her nursing agency. And due to the elevation in her business, she found herself getting less and less sleep. Work during the day and school at night was not the best recipe for sleep or self-care. She was starting to see the effects of her sleep deprivation in her daily life more and more.

"I can't really explain it. It was almost like he was looking through me," Giselle said with a puzzled look on her face as she recanted the event out loud. "I remember sitting at the table, waiting for a friend who had texted me inviting me to meet up for lunch. Shortly after, this guy walks in and sits at the table across from me. At first, I didn't pay him any mind.

I sat texting my friend repeatedly, but she never showed up. After about twenty minutes with no response, I decided to order. I glanced up after the waiter walked away and noticed the man sitting at the table staring at me with this predatory glare. It creeped me out. Not just the staring, but the fact he didn't look away after I met his glance. Most people would just glance away or look down, but not him. Instead, he kept looking at me as if he wanted me to notice him staring at me with his creepy beady little eyes," Giselle explained.

"After sitting at the table and realizing his creepy stares were not going to stop, I decided to leave the restaurant. On my way home, I kept feeling like I was being followed. However, when I looked around I didn't see anyone. This has been going on all week." "Girl, he probably was staring at that big ass designer bag, trying to figure out if there was a big ass wallet filled with money in there to go with it!" Tamra said as she took notice of Giselle's attire. Giselle didn't laugh. "I'd be following you around too," Tamra continued as she dished out her moderately funny jokes trying to get Giselle to losin' up.

"This is why I keep telling you to find yourself a nice guy and start dating. You are too young to be so stiff and unfriendly," Tamra said again as she began to cackle loudly, feeling extremely amused by her joke and insult to her cousin who did not appear to find the comment amusing at all. "I'm fine," Giselle said, "I don't need a man. I can take care of myself." "I know, Miss Independent," Tamra replied sarcastically. "I'm sure you can take care of yourself. We all can, but wouldn't it be nice to have someone around looking out for you? Then, maybe, creepy guys in restaurants wouldn't stare so hard, and you wouldn't be feeling like you're being followed."

Giselle couldn't help but take in a little of what Tamra was saying to her. Her method wasn't the best, but she thought about the possibility of dating and finding someone who could have her back. Yet, the thought of being booed up repulsed her due to her previous encounters with young men.

She was up and functioning off of four hours of sleep; eight hours of sleep total for the last two days. There was no way she was thinking clearly. Sure, the guy creeped her out at the restaurant. She was starting to feel like there was a possibility she was letting her imagination run wild due to her lack of sleep.

Giselle was five feet tall, with a sharp fashion sense, and a revolving door of hairstyles that never seemed to stay the same for long. Tamra could see why a man or men would take notice of the pint-sized educated beauty. What she didn't understand is why Giselle never showed much interest back in anyone. Or why she didn't understand that advances towards someone like her was a common place.

Maybe this was just a rationalization for this weird occurrence with the creepy man. Giselle preferred to keep her nose buried in her books and her mind focused on her business that was currently growing at a much faster pace than what she had anticipated. Between juggling school and work, Giselle often felt tired and overwhelmed due to her lack of sufficient sleep. She would place sleep at the top of her self-care checklist, and then abandon it soon after.

Giselle was not the normal twenty something. She made it no secret that she had no desire to be. For it was this very attitude that made her a constant topic of discussion amongst her constituents. The men her age all thought she was beautiful and stuck up, and the woman all thought she was ambitious, superficial, and self-absorbed. Giselle preferred to live a life of solace, keeping to herself and focusing her energy on her endeavors. This made her not very relatable to the men and women her age. But, it was a quality she had no intention of changing.

Tamra had commented on Giselle's loner lifestyle many times. Each time, touching on ways Giselle could switch it up to find a healthier balance. And, each time she watched as Giselle completely ignored her advice. Giselle was smart, but often too smart for her own good. She had trouble taking the advice of others, feeling like her way was always the best way. However, this would be a character flaw she would soon realize needed polishing.

Tamra was one of the best hair stylists in the city of Richmond,

Virginia. If there was a cut, sew-in, or wig that needed laying, she was the Queen of Slay; earning herself a handsome living working from home, slaying the local heads in her area, earning her quite the reputation as a local stylist. Tamra took notice of Giselle's frontal that appeared to be extremely lifted in the front causing her to be disturbed.

Giselle was still sitting giving Tamra the rundown on the different crazy occurrences she had experienced throughout the week. Tamra tried to listen actively, taking notice of the disassembled lace front more and more as the conversation continued. Finally, feeling as if she could no longer fight the urge to speak up, "Girl, who in the hell laid that wig?" Tamra asked, knowing what Giselle's response would be. "Rocky did it for me last week," Giselle said. She appeared to be completely unaware of the botched job Rocky had done.

"Girl, I told you to stop letting that girl touch your head when she doesn't know what the hell she is doing. There is no way a client is going to walk in here, get a wig, and need a new install a week later," Tamra said. She made sure to let Giselle know, once again, that she didn't approve of her hairstylist. "Selle, go sit in the chair so I can get you together. I cannot have my cousin walking around as a business-woman making deals with clients looking like a plucked chicken," Tamra continued.

She was highly offended that Rocky was still conducting business in her new shop with clients who came out looking like Giselle did. It was things like this that made Tamra upset. She had been doing hair in the city for just as long as Rocky. Yet, Rocky was the one with the shop. Rocky had lucked up and found her a "Money Man," as Tamra liked to refer to him. He purchased her a shop in the city a year ago.

This move led Rocky to believe she was better than Tamra sparking a divide in their once solid friendship leading them to part ways.

Giselle sat in the chair, prepared for one of Tamra's rants about how horrible Rocky did hair. Tamra began the removal process to deinstall Giselle's frontal. As Giselle sat in the chair, she was still in deep thought about the footsteps she had heard approaching her on her way to Tamra's apartment. She recalled how loud the steps were. Was it all in her mind? Or was she being followed?

Tamra kept babbling on and on about Rocky in the background as she attempted to undo and outdo Rocky's work. Giselle thought about the look on the man's face as he sat at the table staring at her. She remembered the look in his eyes. It was a look she had not seen anywhere before except for in the horror films she liked to watch at night, when she was home alone and couldn't sleep. There was something about the man that screamed serial rapist to her as she recalled his face in the back of her memory.

"You know what I'm saying?" Tamra asked as she made her way through the top of Giselle's head, undoing the cornrolls that in her opinion were entirely too big. Giselle did not respond. She was wrapped in her trance, thinking about the creepy man and his intentions for his continuous glares. "Selle, hellooooooo earth to Selle. Is anybody home?" Tamra asked after realizing she was having a full conversation with herself.

"I'm sorry, Tam. I was in a daze," Giselle said as if she hadn't noticed how obvious it was to Tamra that she was and had been a million miles away all night. "Girl, I don't know what's going on with you, but you need to get it together. You're running around thinking you're being followed, your wig looks like it's been installed by a five-year-old, and you look like you haven't had sleep in days. This is clearly not the boss moves you need to be making," Tamra concluded.

Giselle hated hearing Tamra's critiques mostly because she knew she was right. She had gone off a ledge and hadn't looked back. Giselle tried her best to stay on top of her busy daily schedule. It was becoming harder and harder to do and it was starting to show up in other aspects of her life.

Tamra went to the back of her room to grab the items she needed to do a new installation for Giselle. Tamra's phone began to ring repeatedly, breaking Giselle's thought pattern. The sound of the ring tone ended the mental obsession she was enthralled in while letting the day's events replay over and over in her mind. Giselle glanced at the caller I.D. noticing it was Lamont. She rolled her eyes and felt an instant sensation of disgust. Here she was sitting in Tamra's chair listening to her give her piles of advice while she was still engaging in a relationship with one of the most infamous local womanizers the city of Richmond had ever known.

Giselle referred to the relationship between Lamont and Tamra as a situationship. She always felt it lacked the healthy components to be considered a real relationship. Lamont did whatever he wanted to do, when he wanted to do it. Tamra often heard the tales of Lamont's secret counterparts overlooking them, telling herself it didn't matter, because she was the one he always came back to.

She never owned up to the fact that she was the one he always came back to, because she was the only one willing to let him halfway commit. This was something Giselle never understood about her cousin. She had always looked up to Tamra, and felt she could be with any guy she wanted. She didn't understand what was keeping her glued to Lamont's half-truths and efforts. However, she knew not to question Tamra. So, instead, she stayed silent and observed from the sidelines along with everyone else.

Tamra finally came back with the supplies. She sat them out on the table in the order she planned to use them. She glanced at her phone and noticed the missed call from Lamont. Giselle wanted to know what was going on between Tamra and Lamont, after being told on the last visit that she was no longer in communication with him. Which never seemed to last long given their history of this back and forth, off again, on again type of relationship.

"So, what's the latest with you and Lamont?" Giselle asked. "Girl, I don't know how to explain it. But, you know how that goes," Tamra said. She wanted to avoid dishing out full details of their relationship status. Giselle nodded her head and hid her disappointment. Tamra could do a lot better in her opinion, but who was she to judge.

Tamra got to work on Giselle's head and watched her phone ring back-to-back. Twenty minutes later, her screen had become flooded with missed calls from the self-proclaimed local ladies' man who Giselle was certain was not right for her cousin.

"Girl, he is blowing your phone upppp!"Giselle said. She was shocked after seeing how Lamont liked to conduct himself in public. He appeared to everyone else to not have a care in the world that related to Tamra. "Girl, he always does this when I'm not talking to him. Give a man a little attention and they'll treat it like it's worthless. As soon as you start ignoring them that's when they always want to give you the attention you rightfully deserve," Tamra said as she put the finishing touches on Giselle's wig installation.

Tamra turned on the vanity lights, spinning Giselle's chair around ready to let her see the magic she had created on what was once a poorly installed frontal. Giselle glanced in the mirror, falling in love with her new flowy voluminous install. "Girl you did that!" Giselle said as she ran her fingers through the wig, falling in love with the lace concealer Tamra had used making the wig appear to be her natural hair. "Girl, I can't even lie. You are a beast with the install," Giselle said. She took notice of how different Tamra's installation was compared to Rocky's.

Rocky and Tamra were definitely in two different arenas when it came to doing hair. Although Giselle hated admitting it, after being one of Rocky's long-term clients, it was clear that Rocky had nothing on Tamra's slay credibility.

Tamra smiled as she watched her cousin flip and fondle her new hairstyle. There was nothing like seeing a happy client. For Tamra, this was her life's joy. Especially when the customer was one of Rocky's clients. This gave her an extra sense of worth and she didn't try hiding it.

"Cousin, I told you to stop letting that girl put her ashy little hands on your head. Now you see what a real hairstylist can do," Tamra said in her petty tone, still submitting the glow of happiness after seeing how Giselle responded to the new look. "This is how you should be looking when you're out there trying to build up new clientele. No one wants to entrust a young woman with a nappy wig to take care of or find nurse placement for their family member," Tamra said as she continued to chime in on the horrible hair job Rocky had done. Giselle knew she was not going to give it a rest due to her strong dislike for Rocky.

Giselle looked in the mirror while she played in her hair. She loved the voluminous curls. She couldn't help but admit that Tamra may have been right about her bad choice in a hairstylist. "Girl, all I want to know is...what lace?" Giselle asked, smiling and flipping her hair from side to side. "Yesss, cousin. New hair. Who dis?" Tamra added as she gazed at the wonderful job she had done in a short amount of time.

There was something about going to get a new do that made a woman forget about all of her worries. Just like that Giselle had forgotten about everything plaguing her, and all she could focus on was her new jaw-dropping look. Tamra was many things, but no one could take away the fact that she knew how to bless a head in no time.

"Why don't you spend the night?" Tamra asked. "I have to.....,"Giselle attempted before being cut off. "Girl, work will be there tomorrow. Besides, I just laid your wig for free. The least you can do is stay over, and we can have a girl's night like in the old days before you started bossing up and losing out on all the fun."

Giselle had a list of things she had planned to get done during the night when sleep was unattainable. She had a list of edits for her school papers, invoices, and new client inquiries she wanted to get sent out. She felt guilty, and recognized she was being self-absorbed again!

Tamra had helped her with her hair problem so the least she could do was return the favor through girl talk and a night filled with fun gossip and snack binging. Giselle agreed and tried to put the never ending to-do list out of her mind. She had bossed up and felt burnt out. So, for the night, it would be her, Tamra, and her new lace installation! After all, there was no way, she could blow off her cousin after doing such a good job to her hair. In a matter of less than thirty minutes, she had gone from lifted lace to what lace? That was certainly a good enough excuse to abandon a night of work and have some much needed one on one time with her favorite cousin.

5

What Happens in Bali Stays in Bali

Black sat at her table consuming the Ayam Betutu. She had tried a few good meals during her time in Bali, but the Balinese spiced chicken was one of her favorites. Because of what life had thrown at her, it had taken her a while to regain her appetite. Every time she closed her eyes, she saw images of her brother Kenneth and her nieces, Kendall and Kennedy. She had spent her career as a special agent, running into one dangerous situation after another. However, she never thought the dangerous realms she entered and exited, so candidly, would find their way into her family life.

She took in a fork full of the spiced chicken. She attempted to drown out her thoughts of Kenneth and the girls. Black took in the spicy tasteful aroma and swallowed her bites quickly before her agony took over and redirected her appetite.

After months of depression and therapy, Black had finally reached a place where she felt she learned to accept the loss of her family.

Nevertheless, she was in no way ready to walk away from the tragic event without implementing her own form of redemption.

Once she had closed in on the Ramona family and got as close as she could, her cover was blown, her family murdered, and her drive completely exterminated. She had never had her identity revealed in all her ten years as an agent. There was no doubt in her mind that the Ramona family had someone working on the inside. An agent had blown her cover, and she was sure of it. After making a list and narrowing it down to one, she spent the past five months tracking and following the agent she was sure was responsible, Jimmy Gardega. Gardega had been a special agent for twenty-five years. He entered the bureau as a young man who came from humble beginnings.

He had been working undercover as an inside resource for the Ramona family since his third year as an agent. The Ramona family approached him, during his third year as an agent, with a generous offer and salary he could not refuse. Gardega had given the Ramona crime syndicate the intel that helped them to learn Black's true identity, and locate and kill her loved ones.

Gardega knew this was something that, if found out, could get him killed. He waited a few weeks for the dust to settle after the media coverage and ongoing investigation began to die down. Shortly after the smoke diminished, he decided to announce his early retirement.

Gardega packed up and relocated to Bali. He sent out communications telling everyone he and his family had decided to take an overextended vacation in honor of his retirement. For it was this very communication that led Black to Gardega with no trouble. Black had been staying in a hotel that was a little lower than her pay grade.

She wanted to lay low in hopes she would not draw any attention to herself, or be spotted by Gardega or one of his self-entitled money-grubbing sidekicks.

The Balinese-style village hotel Black had selected was just the place to lay low and plot her plans for vengeance. While Gardega was enjoying the good life spending the money he had accumulated through his corrupt actions, Black had been laying low plotting her approach to give him the fate she felt he rightfully deserved.

She had spent her entire life sailing on the right side of the tracks and taking pride in that. She never would have imagined she'd end up anywhere else in life. Unfortunately, tragedy has a way of changing you internally. Black took in the last bite of the spiced chicken before she realized her appetite had fled completely. She had consumed herself with visions of her family's tragic murder. She pictured how Gardega might have had them executed. She would always envision the worst styles of torture and turmoil. This was often what stripped Black of the ability to consume a full meal.

Black exited from the table and scraped the large contents of food into the wastebasket. How could she ever take in a proper meal, knowing that Gardega was somewhere cruising on a yacht, living his best life? While she was left brotherless, drowning in agony from the absence of the only family she had left.

Black broke away from her grief and anger flooded her thoughts. Every time she thought about Kenneth and the girls, she pictured herself ripping Gardega's head off. She knew she could not let her emotions get the best of her. For now, she would stick to her plan. When the time was right, she would do what she needed to do to honor her family, and get the justice she knew would never be served in the real world.

Black slipped into her cropped jeans, white tee, and a baseball cap that said, "When in Bali.'" She wasn't one to dress noticeably. In fact, her entire wardrobe consisted of solid-colored tees, jeans and sweats. This was the best attempt Black could make at appearing to be inconspicuous.

She exited the room and hopped onto the bike she had rented. She knew where Gardega would be spending his day and was going to make every effort to tail him the entire day. This was her mechanism that had helped her track and capture many top-notch experienced criminals. Surely, she would have no trouble with Gardega, so she had assumed.

Unbeknownst to her, she would be interrupted along the way. Black approached the Balinese outdoor market, where she was sure Gardega would be for the first half of his morning. She had been tailing Gardega daily for two weeks after her arrival in Bali. She had become quite familiar with his whereabouts on a daily basis.

Black grabbed some items from her bike basket and proceeded to walk around the market. She appeared to be just another tourist enjoying fresh foods and handmade goods. Black walked around the market for over an hour with no sign of Gardega or his goons anywhere in sight. But how? This was an odd occurrence. Surely, she had not miscalculated the probability of his arrival. She had followed him to the market daily.

No one knew about her mission besides her. She had no family, and work was her only friend. How could Gardega know of her existence without a source? This time Black could be sure there was no source. Yet, there was no sight of Gardega. Maybe he's running late, she thought to herself. Maybe I should just sit here and wait. He'll show, she continued telling herself while making sense of the break in his scheduled routine.

Black sat at the market side table holding her book, glaring up and scanning her environment with each passing minute. There was no way she had come this far and lost her target. She sat for two hours. But, there was still no sign of Gardega.

She felt extremely agitated. Where could he be? She thought while mapping out his schedule in her mind, making sure she had not missed anything. However, nothing was adding up any differently. She retrieved her items, and hopped back on her bike headed for her hotel room. She would need to regather herself and go back to the drawing board.

If Gardega had suddenly changed his routine, there had to be a good reason. She was determined to get to the bottom of what that reason could be. There was no way she was going to let Gardega slip out of her reach without getting the revenge she felt she rightfully deserved.

Black hated feeling like this. Her emotions were out of orbit and her aggression was piling up on the inside. This caused her to feel like a volcano waiting to erupt. It angered her that she had lost her family, Gardega was the cause of her loss, and that he could potentially be aware of her presence in Bali.

When Black's emotions rose to the surface in such a quick manner, it made it hard for her to think clearly. Suddenly, her thoughts and feelings became annoyingly intrusive, making it hard for her to keep her focus. Black hopped off her bike near a secluded wooded area. She grabbed her head on both sides, panting back and forth. She was having an emotional meltdown. She wanted to scream. She needed to scream.

She battled with the fact that she had wanted so badly to be a part of the secret agent world that she had made it her focus. Prior to the death of her family, her brother and nieces had not laid eyes on her for two years. Not because they didn't want to, but because Black had never taken the time to visit them after going undercover back-to-back fueling her selfish ambitious attempts to infiltrate as many well-known crime syndicates possible to spring her career further ahead. Black couldn't help but feel that her family's death was her fault.

She had spent many of her days fueled by the thought of success. There was no way she could have imagined that the very success she was gaining would be the double-edged sword that would rip away the only people she had left in the world. The tears began to fall while Black paced back and forth. She still felt the urge to scream, explode, and evaporate from all existence. Without Kenneth and the girls, she felt like her life was worthless. She wanted to turn back the hands of time and make it all go away, but she couldn't.

Gardega had ripped her entire world from under her feet. It left her mentally stagnated with nothing on her radar, but revenge. Revenge that would lead her to a place of temporary solace while she actively engaged in the very monstrosities that she persecuted others for.

Black screamed, disturbing all the birds nearby. She let her tears compile while she watched the birds fly away in flocks. She dropped to her knees feeling eternally defeated. There it was. The rage, distress, and heartbreak she had been holding in for months now. It all came roaring out loudly at once, draining her slowly while she cried out into the wilderness with no one to comfort her. The outpour of emotion could no longer be contained.

While Black remained frozen in emotions, a black SUV began to approach her followed by several others. Black knew her moment had come. She picked herself up quickly, plunging into the woods, running as fast as she could. She didn't know if she would be able to outrun her assailants, but she had to try.

She shot through the woods, making her way through the Indonesian forest. She could hear the assailants on foot, approaching her as she continued to try and make her escape. She came upon a waterfall. She listened for the footsteps that grew closer and closer. Black looked down, assessing the high drop.

Commander Silver ran with his troops closely behind him. Silver had done his background research on Black. He learned she was quite the quick and intelligent escape artist. "I think she went that way!" Silver yelled, sending the troops in the opposite direction. Silver had become an opportunist. He sought a higher position amongst the elite members of the Illuminus Society. Surely, he would be promoted after his capture and influence in inducting one of the FBI's top agents, he thought to himself as he probed through the forest slowly.

He quietly took notice of the animals that roamed freely through the wild habitat. Black darted out of a nearby bush, kicking Silver in the side of the face, and disarmed him of his gun. Silver fell to the ground. He felt the sting of shock while the right side of his face began to rattle. He tried to reach for the gun, but Black kicked it further away.

"Who are you?" she asked while getting a good look at his attire. Silver was dressed in an all-black trooper style uniform that had no symbols or logos indicating what or who he was representing. Silver gave no reply. Black debated quickly what she should do next, fearing her next move could potentially be her last. She glared at the man dressed in the troop uniform. If her cover had been blown, there was no way she was going to leave Bali alive.

She glanced at the gun, and then back at Silver. This had to be a hired gun sent by Gardega, she thought to herself as she debated whether to kill Silver or let him go. "You don't want to do this!" Silver yelled out in a begging tone filled with fear. "I'm not here to hurt you," he continued. "I'm here to offer you the opportunity of a lifetime." Black looked at Silver, assessing the honesty in his eyes and the fear in his voice. He was telling her the truth. But, why or how she did not understand. Why would an army of men be chasing her through the forest in Indonesia? Why had they traveled all this way for her?

"Come with us. There is someone who will explain it all", Silver said. "Explain what?" Black asked while keeping Silver pinned to the ground. "I am a representative of the Illuminus Society. We are a group of elite African-Americans who are always on the lookout for other African-Americans who have exceptionalities like yourself. We've been studying you for a while," Silver continued.

"Studying me? What the hell do you mean studying me?" She asked not understanding why someone would find her interesting in the way Silver had described. "Yes, we've been studying you, because we feel you would be a perfect fit for our society," he replied. "You tracked me down, came all this way, and chased me through the woods to offer me an invitation to a cult?" Black questioned to make it all make sense.

"It's not a cult," Silver replied. It's a secret society for black excellence. The Illuminus Society has the power and resources to get you to any place of success you desire," he continued. He tried to prey on Black's desires and ambitious motives. "A cult," Black repeated. "I think I'll pass. I have bigger fish to fry, and secret societies aren't quite my lane".

Black left Silver planted on the ground as she made a run for the waterfall. "Wait!" Silver yelled, but she continued running. Surely she wasn't crazy enough to jump, he thought to himself as he watched her in amazement. Black dived into the waterfall plummeting into the water.

Under normal circumstances, Silver would have expected that after a jump like that the person would have perished. But he knew Black was not the average person. Nor was she the average woman. If he was going to have a hand in influencing her to join the Illuminus Society, he was going to have to learn to be diligent, convincing, and quick on his feet. Today, he had been taken down by a woman and there was no way he was going to allow that to happen again. Next time he encountered Karen Black, he would be prepared.

The troops approached Silver as they watched him pull himself up from the ground where he had been for the past few minutes. Kyle Hayden, a troop member who had been inducted into the society two years ago, rushed forth to lend Silver a hand eagerly. "I'm good,"

Silver said sternly, pushing away Hayden's hand as he brushed the debris from his uniform. "Did you find her?" Silver asked. He was aware that they had not. He hid his uncomfortable encounter with Black away from the other troops.

Hayden looked at Silver, sensing he was keeping something from the rest of the group. "No sir, we did not," Hayden replied. "We searched the far-left region of the forest, and saw no sign of her anywhere," Hayden continued as he looked Silver up and down.

Hayden was a new trooper, but a very intuitive one. He was certain Silver had encountered Black, and she had somehow managed to get-away. Silver gave the troops orders to exit the forest and head back to their vehicles.

Hayden staggered behind while he watched the troops make their way to the vehicles. "Sir," Hayden said to get Silver's attention. "Yes," Silver replied reluctantly as he failed to turn around and give Hayden his direct attention. "Where did she go?" Hayden asked. Silver turned around after feeling the shock of Hayden's implications. "Where did she go?" Hayden asked again, this time making it clear in his tone that he was aware of Silver's direct contact with Black.

Silver thought about the best way to respond. He debated on whether he should continue with his lie, or let the young trooper in on what had taken place between him and Black. Hayden had been keeping a close watch on Silver. Silver had started to take notice of the young man's ambition. If he were going to move on from being the commander of the troops, he would need someone he could rely on to take his place. There was no way Queen Mother would ever consider a promotion if Silver had no one in mind that could do his job as well as him.

Silver instantly saw an opportunity. Letting Hayden in on his short-coming would be the perfect opening act to gain his trust he thought to himself. "She got me down on the ground," Silver said, letting his shame be present. "I told her who I was and why we were tailing her. After she refused our offer, she dived into the waterfall and there was no sign of her after that." Silver said, appearing to be crushed at his failed attempt to win Black over with his offer into the Illuminus Society.

Hayden looked at Silver, feeling uncertain of what to say. "I'm sorry she got away, sir," he replied. "It's okay, son. It happens to the best of us. Hayden, I need you to promise me something," Silver continued silently, putting his plan into motion. "I need you to promise me that you will keep this between us. If Queen Mother knew I had Black in my grasp and let her get away, she'd be upset," he concluded. Hayden agreed innocently out of pure admiration for commander Silver.

"Your secret is safe with me, sir," he replied.

"You know what they say, son. What happens in Bali, stays in Bali," Silver replied as he made his way closer to the vehicle for departure. Hayden smiled as he nodded his head. Silver knew he could be certain that Hayden would keep his secret, and this would help him implement his plan to move up in the Illuminus world of secrets and succession.

6

Finding Elizabeth

Elizabeth lay in bed restless unable to break away from the stressors of her chaotic work life that had absolutely no balance. Her regular day-to-day life was starting to feel nonexistent. She had canceled two dates, a nail appointment, and her normal weekly float meditation session. There was something about relaxing in a pod full of water that felt rejuvenating to her after the day-to-day stressors of working in a male-dominated field that was starting to drive her insane.

Elizabeth couldn't help but replay the Bronson account issues over and over in her mind. She felt as though her co-workers were now preying on her peace. They were secretly trying to push her out of the door. She thought about how different her life would be if she were a white woman working for the World and Trust Bank. She hated pulling the race card, but she found it extremely annoying and biased that she was the only person being mistreated.

Elizabeth believed showing up daily to the office as a woman of color was crippling her. She had always felt as though her melanated skin was her most beautiful feature, but now she wasn't so sure. There was no way she could ignore the fact that she was the only person of color in the entire facility. It had been over a year since she had become registered in her field. Yet, she was the only individual not receiving a commission.

Her days had been filled with phone calls from her superiors. Every call led her to a never-ending to-do list that she executed efficiently. However, somehow the conversation about her pay increase had not been addressed. She walked through the office overhearing her constituents brag and boast about their raises and how they were receiving their commission after becoming registered. Still, no one had considered giving her the same courtesy.

What was it about being a black woman in corporate America that made others assume this type of behavior could be deemed permissible? This was a question she silently asked herself as she became more and more consumed by her thoughts. She had been railroaded with the Bronson account, but she somehow managed to get caught up, leaving her oppressors filled with irritation and surprise because they did not think she would be capable of doing so.

Elizabeth thought about her life in New York, and how things were significantly calmer and peaceful in her career in comparison to where she was now. She had left so much behind. She walked unconsciously into a space of disappointment and disapproval. She constantly felt the ironic undertones of her past life chiming in when her miserable thought process took over. How was it possible that she had been more at peace in a fast-paced big city, than in the humble small city she had grown up in? She wondered and tried to make it all make sense.

Elizabeth often turned new corners and faced new forms of ridicule that caused her to feel as though she couldn't do anything right. Her confident, reliable boss personality had been left on the streets of New York. Elizabeth had now become a secluded, self-doubter, spending her days stuck in the house with a cat, a veggie bowl, and a T.V. subscription being her only hobbies, outside of feeling sorry for herself. On nights like this, she wished she could call Jonathan and pull him away from the sleep she was certain he wasn't getting as well.

Ever since his relationship with Alicia started to progress, Elizabeth felt the urge to pull back on her amount of contact. She wanted to keep most of the contact between her and Jonathan during their work hours. This way Alicia wouldn't feel uncomfortable with their relationship. Jonathan had never disclosed to Elizabeth how Alicia felt about her. But, Alicia made it no secret with her uncomfortable facial expressions taking over the room anytime Elizabeth was present.

The phone rang, breaking Elizabeth's mental rant. It was Maddox. Maybe he had received her email and was ready to give her the commission he and all the other team members knew she deserved. Maddox was the only Financial Advisor that felt it was appropriate to contact people at odd hours of the night. He was self-absorbed and full of it; nothing mattered to him. He made it no secret to his constituents that his life revolved around numbers. As long as the numbers looked good, he felt good. Anything outside of that was irrelevant to him. He declined any inquiring about potential clients who had less than five million in their accounts.

"Hello," Elizabeth said as she picked up the phone, feeling a lump forming in her throat. She prepared herself for another uncomfortable conversation. "Hey Beth," he said, giving her a nickname for the first time. Elizabeth felt annoyed. Since when do you refer to me as Beth, she thought silently in her head. "Hey, Maddox," she responded as she put on her poker face implementing her fake happy tone. She knew deep down inside she was anything but happy when hearing the sound of his voice.

"I got your email and the guys and I have talked. We would like to have a meeting tomorrow to discuss the terms of your commission. If you could meet us first thing in the morning around nine a.m., we'd love to have a chat and get the ball rolling," he concluded. Elizabeth felt instant relief. This was the first conversation she had ever experienced with Maddox where he wasn't being a full-blown prick.

She agreed and said goodbye. Elizabeth felt the excitement of progress. She had chosen to take the high road, fighting off the urge to say the things she was feeling towards her co-workers daily. Finally, she was going to receive what she had hoped for, fairness. Elizabeth picked up the phone to call Jonathan to give him the good news. The phone rang repeatedly, but there was no answer. While Elizabeth attempted to get a hold of Jonathan to tell him the good news, Jonathan was experiencing his own issues.

Jonathan's phone rang over and over, waking him from his sleep. Alicia hopped up, grabbing the phone as if she had designated rights to it. "What are you doing?" Jonathan asked, still not fully awake while wiping the debris from his eyes. "Why is she calling you at this time of the night?" Alicia questioned with a look of disapproval plastered all over her face. Jonathan was not in the mood for Alicia's jealous oriented antics. Elizabeth was not one to disrespect the origins of their relationship. So, he knew if she was calling outside of their normal chatting hours, it had to be for an important reason.

Jonathan grabbed the phone abruptly ready to exit the room. He avoided the conversation about how inappropriate it was for Elizabeth to be calling. He retired from the room, and left Alicia's side as he walked away from the continued conversation that consisted of nothing but jealousy and negativity. The more Jonathan heard Alicia speak, the more aggravated he was starting to become with her.

Alicia sat in the bed feeling disturbed. She was starting to feel like Elizabeth loved playing the role of the damsel in distress. It was also starting to appear to her that Jonathan loved the dynamic as well. He was a psychiatrist, but that didn't make him everyone's designated psychiatrist in his circle of friends, she thought frustratedly to herself.

She had questioned the nature of Jonathan and Elizabeth's friendship many times before. Each time being assured that nothing was going on. This however did not appear to be the "nothing going on" aspect she had been previously assured of. Alicia was certain that Jonathan departing from the bedroom in the manner he did was more of a something than a nothing. Her friends were all starting to make her feel like she was the jealous suspicious partner. But clearly, something was going on.

Jonathan waited until he heard Alicia's complaints die down. He waited eagerly on the other end for Elizabeth to answer, but she did not. He prayed silently to himself that all was well, fearing the worse. What if she was having a nervous breakdown, he thought to himself. Surely, she had become fed up with life and her circumstances by now, he assumed.

Maybe I should drive over and check on her, he thought. Overlooking the jealous fiancé' that lay waiting for him in the other room. Although he hated to analyze and admit it to himself, Jonathan was starting to become more aware of his feelings for Elizabeth. He found it disturbing that he cared more about Elizabeth at the current moment than Alicia.

The cell phone chimed, alerting him of a text notification. "Sorry to disturb you so late," the text read. "I wanted to let you know Maddox reached out in response to the email you helped me prepare. It looks like it worked! I have a sit-down scheduled for tomorrow morning with all of the FA's! Looks like your girl is going to get that money!!!" Jonathan smiled, feeling relieved that it was good news. "Get that money," he said in a reply text.

He felt happy for Elizabeth and debated on whether he should rejoin Alicia in the bedroom or remain on the sofa. He thought back assessing her choice of words, allowing the insults towards his friend to replay in his mind over and over. Alicia was well established and grew up extremely privileged. Jonathan often felt her lack of struggle made it hard for him to relate to her in many ways that mattered to him personally. He also felt her high maintenance lifestyle often made her feel superior to most black women who didn't have what she had. This was a quality he hated about her.

The sofa would be his final resting place for the night. He grabbed a duvet and pillow from the linen closet and made himself comfortable. He reminisced about how far he and Elizabeth had come together in their friendship journey. It felt like it was yesterday that they were both kids working at the local ice cream shop together. He recalled a memory of those days drifting off into pure bliss as he took a stroll down memory lane.

Jonathan stood at the counter feeling the urge to want to clock out shortly after arriving to work. His boss, Mr. Nadar, pulled up to the front of the store in his luxury vehicle. He stepped out prepared to critique any and all issues he spotted within the first few seconds of his arrival. "Tuck your shirt in, and put a smile on your face!" he yelled as he walked through the door. "At least pretend like you're happy to be here," he said as he focused his attention on Jonathan. Jonathan didn't know which he hated more. His job or his boss. Most days it felt like an even tossup.

"There's a new girl starting today. I want her to be the designated ice cream maker for the weekends. I want you to train her, Jonathan," Mr. Nadar insisted. "She is nice, smart, and knows how to follow directions. Unlike some of the rest of you! I am a close friend of her mother. So, I want you all to be polite and helpful. Jonathan, I want you to train her properly." Jonathan stood quietly not giving a reply.

The last thing he needed was another clueless teenager following him around. Jonathan in grown man form was intelligent, diligent, and caring, but teenage Jonathan was the total opposite. Teenage Jonathan was lazy, self-absorbed, and sarcastic.

He agreed to train the new girl, feeling annoyed and ready to make a comment he knew would most likely get him into trouble with Mr. Nadar. Teenage Jonathan had a problem with keeping his mouth shut during the times he knew keeping his mouth shut was the better option.

Elizabeth walked through the door dressed in her uniform, surprising Jonathan immediately. "Wait, you're the new girl?" he questioned with a huge smile on his face. "Why didn't you tell me you were going to be working here?" he asked. "I thought I'd surprise you. You're always saying how boring work is. So, I thought you'd feel relieved if you had a friend to work with," Elizabeth said with a smile equivalent to Jonathan's on her face. "I'm going to be training you while Mr. Nadar sits on his fat butt and does nothing but yell at us," he said, encouraging a laugh from Elizabeth.

Jonathan's phone chimed again, breaking his stroll down memory lane. "Thanks for always being here for me," the text read. He smiled. "No problem. You know I will always have your back," he replied. As much as he hated to admit it, Elizabeth gave him a feeling no one else did or could. His mother had always hoped the two of them would get together, always sparking a reply of lack of interest from Jonathan.

He felt it deeply embedded in his core. It was like he was floating in his own body fueled high by a euphoric feeling that only seemed to emerge during his time and talks with Elizabeth. Alicia was beautiful, well off, and successful, but she had never made Jonathan feel the way Elizabeth did. He knew she never would. Every day, he was falling into a routine with Alicia that he knew he no longer wanted to be a part of.

Jonathan began assessing his behavior. He took notice of his short responses, lack of affection, and lack of interest in his fiancé. He thought to himself how far he had let things get. Day after day, he'd enter his home and listen to Alicia engage in numerous phone conversations with her loved ones, detailing what would and wouldn't take place at their wedding. It drove Jonathan mad. Alicia was planning for a wedding while he was unconsciously planning for his departure from the relationship.

Why couldn't he come out and say what he knew needed to be said? Why couldn't he look Alicia in the eye, tell her he wasn't in love with her, and he didn't want to marry her? The answer was simple. Alicia, from the beginning of the relationship, invested in Jonathan's endeavors financially, and was the reason he now sat in his own private psychiatric practice business based on the funding from her and her family.

He felt guilty and believed he owed her, because she had done so much for his career and his future. The first week he opened his business, he was contacted by several NBA players and well-known celebrities living in the area based on the word-of-mouth referrals Alicia and her family had been dishing out within their well to do circle of friends.

Jonathan's business had come a long way in a year, and he owed it all to Alicia. He battled with this daily. He often worked up the courage to have a conversation with Alicia, and would change his mind shortly after hearing her talk about plans for the future.

Jonathan turned off his thoughts and positioned himself comfortably on the sofa. Tomorrow, he had his regularly scheduled session with Omari Bronson. He had been thinking about their last session ever since Omari left his office. The Illuminus Society sounded intriguing, and Jonathan was anticipating hearing more.

The alarm clock went off systematically and woke Elizabeth from her sleep. She jumped out of bed suddenly feeling nauseated. Today was a big day! Although she had been awaiting the arrival of the meeting, she felt anxious. She browsed through her closet, looking for what to wear. She retrieved an all-black pants suit, a black satin blouse, and black one-inch kitten heels. Either today would be a step in the right direction, as far as her career was concerned, or it would be the death of all hopes for her potential growth at the World and Trust Bank. Elizabeth felt she should hope for the best, and prepare for the funeral of her career just in case. She brushed her teeth, assessed the bags under her eyes, and felt dissatisfied with her drained facial features.

It was more than apparent to her that her current position with the

World and Trust Bank had been depleting her for quite some time. She paused for a moment, and thought of all the things that could go right during this meeting while considering all the things that could potentially go wrong. Elizabeth needed today to be a good one. So, she pushed aside her negative thoughts, and said a prayer. She was either going to leave the office today with her commission, or she was going to leave with her dignity. Either way, she had made the conscious decision to make today a step in the right direction with or without the backing and support of her constituents.

She got dressed quickly, applied light makeup, and replenished Sprinkle's bowl with dry cat food. Her phone chimed alerting her that she had received a text message. "Good morning, I wanted to wish you good luck before your meeting," the text read. Elizabeth smiled, responding quickly thanking Jonathan for the good morning text and encouragement.

She grabbed her keys and headed for the door. She was filled with anxiety and excitement for the meeting that felt as though it had been a long time coming. It felt good to know she was finally going to get what she felt she deserved. It would place her within the realm of equality amongst her peers.

Elizabeth turned on the radio. She wanted to calm herself down. Her mind was racing, and she felt extremely overwhelmed. She tried to predict how the meeting would go. She plagued herself with thoughts about who would be attending, and who would be commenting when she spoke her piece presenting a sound and solid argument for why she should be receiving a commission.

"Yessssss my song!!!!" Elizabeth yelled as she turned up the volume, after hearing Cardi B's song, "Money" piercing through her car speakers. "I was born to flex, diamonds on my neck, I like boarding jets..." Elizabeth sang to the top of her lungs. "Money...Money...," she continued, feeling the song taking over her thought process as she pushed her worries to the back of her mind regarding the meeting.

Elizabeth approached the bank in her vehicle and turned the music down. The last thing she needed was her co-workers hearing her blasting rap music and placing more stigmas on her. She was tired of feeling like she couldn't be herself and couldn't do anything right. She pulled into her designated parking spot, and began to prepare herself mentally before she entered the building. She closed her eyes and started praying out loud. She wanted to get her positive energy flowing. "Lord, please let this meeting go the way I need it to. Please, please, Lord do not, I repeat do not let Katherine show her face during this meeting, in Jesus' name I pray. Amen!

There was something about the sight of Katherine's smug expressions that made a bad day or an uncertain day feel a lot worse instantaneously. Elizabeth put on her game face entering the building with a confident walk and appearance despite the butterflies that were currently festering in her gut. Today was either going to be the day she made a step in the right direction, or the day she started looking for a new job. She had prepared herself to be okay with either outcome.

She walked into the building noticing the awkward stares from multiple co-workers. "Good Morning to you weirdos, too," she said quietly under breathe, as she smiled at all of the glaring faces and got no response back. She sat at her desk feeling her anxiety returning. She tried to calm herself down. "You got this. You are enough. You are a great woman, and you deserve to be treated equally," she chanted over and over until she felt the affirmations starting to sink in removing her anxiety.

Maddox entered the room, greeting Elizabeth with a bright smile and a hello. "Are you ready for the meeting?" He asked, still filling the room with an expressive glow that Elizabeth found to be unusual. "As ready as I'll ever be," Elizabeth responded. "Is Katherine going to be present at the meeting?" Asked Elizabeth. "No, she called out this morning. Apparently, she isn't feeling well." "Look at God," Elizabeth said under her breath. "What was that?" asked Maddox. "Aww, I'm so sorry. I was hoping she could attend," she said, lying through her teeth. She felt instant relief that her co-worker would not be present to ruin her day as she had done many times before.

Elizabeth grabbed her notepad and walked over to the board room, waiting patiently for the remaining co-workers to arrive. She felt doubtful about what she wanted to say. She also questioned if it was appropriate to bring up the obvious fact that she was the only employee not receiving a commission, who also happened to be the only registered assistant of color.

Maddox entered the room followed by a team. Adam McCallister entered the room last accompanied by Jessica Tomfield who was the supervisor for the World and Trust Bank. Adam had built a successful career for himself as a financial advisor and had been featured in Forbes magazine. He had become accustomed to being viewed as the most diligent of the advisors in his area. He always carried himself with a level of prestige and moderate pretentiousness, entering every room as if he were the superior of superiors.

Elizabeth took a deep breath. She realized no one had made her aware that Adam would be joining the meeting. Jessica took the floor, appearing to want to take the lead. Leading had been something she had failed to do since Elizabeth s arrival. Jessica effortlessly conveyed to her employees that she was a lazy paper pusher who did everything a supervisor should do besides actually supervising.

"I thank you all for coming to this meeting today. We have all been asked to meet, because there is an associate on this team who is not currently receiving commission and Maddox asked us all here to discuss the matter and see what can be done to help progress this individual's career," Jessica said, smiling while making direct eye contact with Elizabeth. "Elizabeth, I would like to first have you make your argument as to why you feel your team should be paying you a commission," said Jessica, taking notice of Elizabeth's discomfort.

Elizabeth stood up, feeling extremely awkward as everyone gave her their attention. "I've asked you all here today, because I wanted to discuss my commission. I was originally told, by Maddox, that I would receive commission after I passed my test, was fully certified, and registered in the required states. I passed my test and some significant time has passed and it has been brought to my attention that I am the only one in this office not receiving a commission," Elizabeth said as she took notice of the glaring eyes, staring her in the face, with disgust as if she had some nerve to point out the obvious. "So, I wanted to bring that to my team's attention so that we could get the ball rolling, and I could get what I deserve," she concluded.

Maddox took the floor after Elizabeth was seated, still smiling from ear to ear. "Although it is a normal gesture to grant an assistant a commission after they have completed the certification process, like you have. I too believe that an individual should receive what they deserve. After speaking with my colleagues and bringing it to their attention, we all feel that you have not yet proved yourself as an assistant. We feel that it is in the fair and best interest of the entire team to have you prove yourself and your capabilities as we had to. The team and I feel that you are still very green in the game and need a significant amount of training. So, we have put together a plan of action we feel would be best to help get you to where you need to be within the next year. Once this training has been implemented properly, we could revisit the discussion of commission within a year's time," Maddox said.

Elizabeth tried to contain her anger and disappointment as she focused her energy on Jessica. She waited patiently for Jessica to chime in and advocate for her as her supervisor and as a woman who could understand how easy it was for a woman to be railroaded in a male-dominated field. However, Jessica said nothing.

The room stood still for five minutes as everyone waited for Elizabeth's response. Elizabeth sat silently, debating if she should respond with her anger, cursing out the entire room that was filled with self-serving individuals who didn't care about her struggles in the world of finance because her struggles were not relatable to them. Or if she should say nothing, pack up her office, and walk away. She thought about what she wanted to say to her co-workers as she arose from her chair calmly. She prayed to God that she didn't merge into the angry black girl they all wanted so desperately for her to be.

"You know when I first arrived here, I was extremely excited.

I remember the day Jessica called me on the phone, giving me my initial interview. I felt accomplished, because I had been offered a job at the infamous World and Trust Bank. That day, I called all of my friends and family telling them the good news. I had trouble organizing my thoughts, because all I could think about was that I, a young black woman, had been offered the job opportunity of a lifetime. I had done my research on Adam, prior to applying here, and all I could think about is that one day that could be me. On the cover of Forbes, in classrooms, and most importantly in low-income communities spreading the knowledge I had gained from being in this field. I envisioned what it would be like the first time I sat down in my office, and what it would be like working with all of you. The first week I came to work I experienced a culture shock, after looking around the room and realizing I was the only one of my kind here."

Maddox stood up abruptly, and made a face shriveling up his nostrils as his face became bloodshot red. Elizabeth glanced at him, giving him a look that made it clear that there would be no interruptions. She was determined to say what needed to be said. He could tell from the look in her eyes his interjection would not be welcome. Maddox sat down quickly nodding to Elizabeth, allowing her to finish.

"I held my head high and told myself that although it was off-putting and unsettling, I could not let it discourage me, and I didn't. I sat through countless conversations where I heard other advisors make inappropriate comments. They frowned their faces at me as I walked by, doubting my ability to my face, and making numerous inappropriate comments about my hairstyle changes. I had co-workers ask me to touch my hair, and being tone-deaf to their approach in conversations with me, the new black woman who was hired to be seen and not heard."

"I sat quietly when I took my test, and didn't receive commission after finding out my counterparts had passed their test and received theirs right away. Rationalizing irrational behavior by telling myself that because I am a black woman I would have to prove myself a little more before receiving what I deserve. But, you know what the problem is with that approach?" Elizabeth asked as she looked around the room at her co-workers, assessing their stunned and anxious facial expressions as they awaited her next comment. "The problem is I'm tired of proving myself to people. Because no matter what I do, it will never be enough in environments like this," she concluded.

The faces of those who made her have feelings of inadequacy, on a daily basis, were filled with shock and shame. Maddox stood up ready to interject, but Elizabeth cut him off. "I'm not done," she said calmly, looking Maddox in the eye with an expression of rage glaring in her eyes as she went on with her calm rant about her uncomfortable experiences while working with them.

"You see, I've entered this building daily, being polite, and understanding. Often trying to put myself in your position, wondering what it is you see when you look at me that makes you want to ignore, discredit, disrespect, and cheat me out of the quality of respect and pay I deserve for the hard work that I do here. You know what I come up with when I think about this?" She asked.

The room stood still and no one replied. Elizabeth looked at Maddox who no longer had the cheerful quirky look plastered on his face he had initially entered the room with. "Do you know what I came up with Maddox?" Elizabeth asked firmly, raising her voice, letting her anger be present in her question. Maddox did not respond. He avoided eye contact with Elizabeth as he held his head down to hide his shame. He felt this way due to Elizabeth's transparent rage that was now coming out as she showed her vulnerable side. She made her co-workers aware of the scars she walked away with daily from the toxic work environment they had become unconsciously okay with cultivating.

"I came up with nothing," she said. Because, I am a human. I am a good human. Unlike most of you in this room, who think it is okay to mistreat the undeserving based on your inflated egos and superficial superior sense of self." Elizabeth concluded.

Elizabeth stood patiently, realizing no one had any feedback for her comments, because they all knew that every word she had spoken was true. She thanked Maddox for the opportunity to work with his team. She exited the room silently, leaving the others still and quiet as they looked around the room assessing each other's guilt-ridden facial expressions. She had never been one to give up, or walk away from adversity. However, it had become clear to her at that moment, that the only opportunity that would be available to her if she stayed in her position would be the opportunity to be overlooked, underpaid, and under appreciated. Elizabeth knew her worth. So, walking away was the only sensible option she felt she had.

Elizabeth pulled a brown box from her work closet. She had stored the box for weeks, keeping it as a just-in-case option for herself if she ever decided to quit. The day had finally come for her to put the box to use. She began clearing the items from the top of her desk, quickly placing her pictures, trinkets, and purse inside of the box. She cleared her desk drawers and exited the office, taking notice of the lack of empathy from her coworkers as they all watched her exit the building without a word. It became clear to her that Maddox had put together the meeting with ill intent.

He had never planned on paying her the commission she had been promised. His goal was to frustrate her by once again railroading her. Stringing her along thinking it was okay to give her less than what she deserved while he piled up her workload, watching her execute boatloads of tasks effectively and efficiently still feeling as though it was his right to treat her in that manner.

No one stopped her on her way out, tried to convince her to stay, or encourage her to cool off and return later. She wondered why she hadn't left months ago. She felt like a fool for having faith that Maddox would do the right thing, only to be slapped in the face by his choice and humiliated in front of everyone.

Elizabeth sat in her car feeling drained. She cried and cried for minutes. There was a tap in the window. Adam McAllister stood on the other side of the window, watching Elizabeth cry while requesting to join her as she sobbed uncontrollably. She tried to get herself together after seeing his face.

Adam entered the car and handed Elizabeth a tissue. He waited patiently for her to expel all of her tears so he could give her the advice he felt she rightfully needed to hear. After hearing her transparent vent about the emotional triggers she had been made to endure during her time at the World and Trust Bank, he felt like he needed to give her words of wisdom.

"Are you finished?" he asked, looking at Elizabeth conveying frustration for her tears. Elizabeth frowned her face. She tried to figure out why the middle-aged Caucasian man had come to her aid if he felt the desire to be rude during her time of struggle. "Why are you giving them your energy?" he questioned with a confused look on his face. Elizabeth's crying started to suppress as she tried to make sense of where Adam was going with his approach to her pain. "I think it was very brave of you today what you said back there. But, I also feel it was very stupid," he continued.

Elizabeth's expression changed as she took offense to Adam's statement. "It wasn't stupid, because they all needed to hear it. They needed to hear it so they could be aware of themselves," she said with animosity taking over her tone and expression. "You don't think they're aware of themselves?" Adam asked rhetorically. "They are aware of how they have been treating you. But, you've allowed it to build up until this point. That's why they continue to do it. They did not see you as an image that is considered the 'industry standard' for what they believe a financial assistant or future advisor is and should look like, so they taunted you," Adam concluded.

"That isn't fair," Elizabeth said. "They may not feel like I fit the 'image,' but I am the image because I do the work," said Elizabeth. "Look around, Elizabeth. We all are doing the work. But, unfortunately, you are entering a world where the standard considered by most in this field is a white male. Unfortunately, anyone entering this world who doesn't fall under those demographics is going to have to put up a fight. No, it's not fair. But, what is in this world," he questioned as he watched Elizabeth take in his words.

Adam continued, "Let me ask you something. Why do you want to be an advisor?" "I want to make great money and learn information about investments and building wealth so I can give back. I want to take this information and spread it in underprivileged communities to teach them how to build generational wealth," Elizabeth said.

"Did your parents build generational wealth for you?" Adam asked Elizabeth in a condescending tone. "No, they did not. That is why I want to help others. I saw early on how their lack of stability affected my future when I stepped out on my own."

"Well, that sounds nice and it's a textbook response that warms people's hearts. But, in reality, you don't see those things taking place in certain communities because those aren't the people investing. Black and brown communities are not out here giving their money to white men that look like me, and trusting they can be led to a better future through market investments."

"No, they're not going to trust a white man. However, they would trust a black woman. Look around there aren't any. Well, maybe they would trust men like your if people like me were allowed to grow in this field instead of being ostracized and overlooked," Elizabeth said.

"You're right, but how can you be that black woman if you give up and walk away," he said, leaving Elizabeth speechless. "I have a good feeling about you Elizabeth. This may not be the place for you, but I'm sure you'll find it. Keep that passion and don't be afraid to put up a fight," Adam said before exiting the car.

Elizabeth drove home irritated the entire ride. She thought about what Adam had said to her about not fitting the industry standard for what a financial representative looked like. As she drove, she began to wonder why she had been spoken to about inclusion during her interview. Yet, she had experienced nothing more than exclusion during her entire time as an employee there.

Elizabeth entered her home with a humdrum demeanor as she took notice of the lazy secluded cat, laying on the sofa uninterested in her arrival. She had experienced a horrible day and had no drive left in her whatsoever to do anything outside of the depressive itinerary she had set up in her head for the remainder of her night. A bubble bath, Netflix, and binge eating junk food would be her nightcap; after the draining day that had made her feel as though she had no real energy left.

Elizabeth undressed and climbed into the hot water filled with Himalayan pink salt and bubbles. She began to relax her tired and aching body. She closed her eyes to relax as much as she could, and tried to think of the best way to move forward. She began to realize it may have been a poor choice to walk away from a job before having another one lined up.

She began to soak, pushing her body deeper into the water until she felt completely comfortable. The bubbles pressed up against her body while her bottom sat embedded in the salt particles as the steam rose from the tub. Elizabeth felt her skin softening as the Himalayan particles hydrated her brown skin, helping her to become mentally somber as she soaked in the tub. She took in the first aura of peace she had experienced all day. She began to drift off, nodding off to sleep.

Elizabeth began walking through a dark space. She was unable to make out anything familiar in her surroundings. She took notice of the tree limbs that appeared to be blowing in the dark wind. An owl sat planted on the limb of a tree, hooting repetitively as he looked at her without breaking his visual. Her white gown blew in the wind as she continued her walk through the gloomy woods. She tried to figure out how it was she had gotten there. She heard a noise in the distance, brushing through the woods fast as if they were running. "Hello, is anyone there?" But there was no response. The owl flew away, leaving her on her own in the dark creepy woods.

Elizabeth's heart started racing. Her anxiety kicked in immediately as she tried to understand how she had gone from her comfortable bathroom setting to a dark low spirited wooded area within seconds. Her skin began to tremble as she watched the goosebumps compile on her forearm. Her body began to shiver uncontrollably. She heard the sound again. This time it sounded like the running was closer in proximity to where she was currently standing. She looked around again, seeing nothing but the countless rows of trees still blowing while the sky became darker filled with stillness.

"Hello, is anyone there?" She asked again. This time fear ran rampant through her tone as her body continued to shiver. Elizabeth felt overwhelmed by the cold that pierced through her thin white nightgown that blew frivolously with the wind as it flowed solemnly throughout the gloomy environment.

"I know someone's there. I can hear you. Come out and show your face." But, there was still no one. She continued to walk and finally spotted a light in the distance. She walked closer to the light until she reached a gated home.

"Hello," she said again and still there was no reply. The home was monumental in size. She could see the lights shining through the curtains from a distance. She tugged at the gate, hoping to make her way in. However, the gate was locked. She noticed an unusual crest, overlapping the bars of the gate. She ran her hands over the steel-plated crest, and tried to make out the images in the dark. The crest began to glow and the images became visible to Elizabeth.

On the front of the crest, she could see a book, a bird, an eye, and an image that appeared to be of a black woman. The crest continued to expel a powerful light that ran through Elizabeth's body. It froze her in place, while the beam of light pierced through the core of her body. The light depreciated, allowing her to move again. She felt an enormous amount of power running through her body that she could not explain. A vision flashed in her mind, giving her a visual of an African-American man she had never seen before. "I have found you daughter, and it is time," he said, smiling and extending a hand to her as the flash abruptly disappeared.

The gates of the mansion began to open slowly, creaking loudly while the cold continued to press up against Elizabeth's body. She entered through the gates reluctantly as she debated if she was making the proper choice. Elizabeth had always been afraid of the dark. It didn't seem like a good idea for her to continue standing out in the unknown while she was tormented by the cold that continuously pierced through her thin gown.

She entered the gates slowly, and made her way to the front of the mansion. She wondered where she was, and who it was that inhabited the beautiful residence. She approached the door. As she prepared to knock, the doors began to open.

Elizabeth was greeted by a well-dressed butler, standing in the door with what appeared to be clothing well folded in his hands. "Welcome, Ms. Smith. We have been expecting you. Here is some warm and comfortable clothing for you to change into," he said as he took notice of the thin gown she had arrived in. "Thank you," she said, as she grabbed the clothing. "You can follow me this way. We have prepared a room for your arrival," the man said, still giving her no real inclination as to where she was and why she was there.

The butler guided Elizabeth to a room, opened the door, and revealed to her the most spacious, elegant room and decor she had ever seen. "If you need something you may summon me. I will retrieve whatever it is you need," the butler said as he prepared to exit the room. Elizabeth stopped him in his tracks before he could completely exit. "Where am I and how do you know my name?" She asked. The butler turned around smiling from ear to ear. "You are at the House of Illuminus," he said. "Illuminus? What is the House of Illuminus, and why am I here?" She asked. "Lord Magnus will be here shortly and he shall explain everything to you," the butler replied, as he closed the door behind himself, leaving Elizabeth to change.

Elizabeth slipped on the pair of silk cream-colored pajamas, with a cream-colored wool robe that had the same crest from the gate plastered on the breast area of the garment. She sat on the bed and tried to make sense of her day. First, the meeting at the World and Trust Bank, and now this, she thought to herself as she heard a light tapping at her door. "May I come in," the voice asked. She paused.

What if she was in danger? She had never heard of the House of Illuminus. Nor did it make any sense to her how she had been soaking in her bathtub drifting off and waking up in the dark woods. She wondered what would happen if she said nothing. Maybe the voice on the other side of the door would go away. But, he did not.

"I know this has to be kind of frightening for you. You showed up here with no clue as to where you are and why you're here," the man said as he spoke through the other side of the door. "If you let me in, I can explain everything. I promise you that you're in a safe place and no one is going to hurt you," the man assured while Elizabeth continued to be silent, assessing the tone of his voice. He didn't sound like a serial killer, but that didn't mean he wasn't one.

Elizabeth cracked the door backing away abruptly. She awaited her fate as she watched the man enter the room. The man was extremely short, with a hunched back and a disfigured facial aesthetic. He entered the room with a solemn demeanor. At first sight, he appeared to be of no harm to Elizabeth at all. "Hello, my name is Magnus," the short funny looking man said as he stood in the middle of the room informally. He tried to get a feel for how he should approach Elizabeth. He could see the fear and uncertainty on her face as she tried to avoid making direct eye contact with him.

"You have been brought here today because you have been selected to be a part of a great organization," said Magnus. "You have a gift that we here at the Illuminus Society feel could be proven to be extremely helpful," the disfigured man continued. "Illuminus Society?" Elizabeth questioned. "Yes, the Illuminus Society," Magnus replied.

He took notice of the young woman's confusion. "I know you

must have a lot of questions. I will be happy to answer them after I've explained why we have summoned you here. The Illuminus Society has been operating in secrecy for many decades. It was created after the abolishment of slavery. A man named Samuel Brown wanted to do something to influence the lifestyles and culture of the struggling black community. He rallied up and brought together the best of the best farmers, educators, and inventors he could find. He traveled by boat, horse, and sometimes foot to spread the word of the black organization he was trying to establish."

Elizabeth was starting to become enthralled with the story although she was still confused. "Samuel gathered as many people as he could to set up secret meetings to take place on the eleventh day of every third month. We have kept this tradition of secret meetings 'til this very day," Magnus stated informatively. "One day, during one of his recruiting voyages, Samuel traveled to the city of New Orleans where he met the infamous Marie Laveau. She was the well-renowned queen of voodoo. Samuel had heard about Maria's abilities from another voodoo specialist named Dr. John Alexander. Dr. Alexander told Samuel that Marie was the perfect person to assist him. So, Samuel paid Marie a visit. Word had spread about her identity and abilities throughout the city. She was the go-to person for any and all who needed things conjured up. Such as money, love, or a miracle in general."

"Samuel arrived at Marie Leveau's home. Where he informed her of his plans to elevate his secret society. Marie gave Samuel special candles along with magic pins and told him to stick the pins in a voodoo doll she had created for him. Marie told Samuel that the red pin signified power, the blue pin signified love, the green pin signified money, the purple pin signified spirituality, and the yellow pin signified success. Samuel took the doll and made his way back to the bed and breakfast where he was staying. Legend has it he waited three days before doing what he was told to do with the doll. On his third day in New Orleans, Samuel decided to set up an altar in his room. He had been instructed by Marie on how to set up the altar and how to properly offer himself to the voodoo spirits. Leveau instructed Samuel to set up the altar only when he was completely ready."

Magnus looked up at Elizabeth, who was now seated on the edge of her bed listening to the story giving him her full attention. It appeared to him that the young woman was now a lot less nervous so he continued with the story. "Samuel had been made aware by the voodoo priestess that the spirits would present themselves to him immediately after setting up the altar if his intentions were pure. She disclosed to him that he should not set up the altar if he had hopes of controlling the spirits or seeking something from them. For if those were his intentions the spirits would not show themselves or offer him anything upon their arrival."

"Leveau expressed to Samuel that the voodoo spirits were all former slaves and did not wish to be controlled. She explained to Samuel that after setting up the altar the spirits would show themselves either allowing him to be accepted and move forward with an ongoing spiritual relationship or rejecting him with violence. Samuel had success after setting up the altar and the spirits showed themselves to him. He started building a relationship with six spirits who presented themselves to him that night at the altar."

"On his eleventh day in New Orleans, he lit the special candles the voodoo queen had given him. The blue candle was to help him possess the power of persuasion. The yellow candle was to help him obtain knowledge and success. The brown candle was to help him obtain material prosperity. The green candle was to help him gain money and wealth, and the gold candle was for love and good luck. Samuel lit all of the candles and a few minutes later the spirits showed themselves to him."

"They again thanked him for his sincerity and promised to help him achieve his goal to cultivate the Illuminus Society. The next day, Samuel left New Orleans and traveled back to Virginia unaware of all of the blessings that awaited him. When he arrived at his home, he was shocked to find that the small beaten-down shack he had been living in was displaced and replaced by a huge home that was enclosed by a large surrounding gate with a crest plastered on the front. The house was filled with crates of money, and a farm filled with live-stock and multiple horses for travel."

"The voodoo spirit Christophe revealed himself to Samuel. The spirit gave Samuel abundance and expressed how pleased all the spirits were with him. Christophe told Samuel that as long as he kept a sincere heart and approach, he and the other spirits would continue to bless him with all that he desired to get the Illuminus Society up and running. Samuel kept his intentions pure concerning his relation-ship with the spirits, and in return, they kept their promise to him," Magnus concluded.

"What does any of this have to do with me?" asked Elizabeth. "The Illuminus Society seeks out the best of the best within the black community. We have some of the world's best scientists, singers, doctors, lawyers, you name it, currently working as members of our society. They are leading the world into progress and excellence. We feel you'd be a great addition to our society. You're great with numbers, and have an ability that could be useful to us here at the House of Illuminus." Elizabeth looked confused. "Ability? What ability are you talking about?" She questioned.

"Do you remember how you got here tonight?" Magnus asked. Elizabeth sat quietly as she tried to think back on how it was that she had arrived at the Illuminus mansion. "I was taking a bath. I remember getting in the bathtub and closing my eyes to relax and...and…I don't know," she replied. "You were summoned here by the spirits. After receiving an invitation from Christophe, you accepted and you arrived by astral projection," Magnus said as he continued to assess Elizabeth's confused state. Elizabeth couldn't believe what she was hearing. "So, you're telling me that I left my body and that's how I got here… There's no way."

"That is correct," Magnus said. He looked at Elizabeth with a straight face. "You've done it many times. Ever since you were a small child about four or five you have been able to do it. At the age of four, when your mother's mother, Nana Smith, as you liked to call her, passed away from a long-term battle with lung cancer you did it," said Magnus.

"I did what?" Elizabeth asked in a rude tone. She started to become annoyed with Magnus as she began to get freaked out. "You projected yourself into the spirit world where you got to spend one last day with your grandmother after she died. You told your mom, but she did not believe you. You don't remember the last time you did it, do you? The day your mother died you projected in your sleep and found her laid in her bed unconscious. You curled up in the bed with her, and you stayed there for two days before you projected back into your body."

Elizabeth began to remember despite the urge of not wanting to. Tears began to flow from her face as she remembered her abilities. She had become scarred and torn by the sight of her mother's still and cold corpse that she had somehow managed to lock out the memory of that day and her abilities altogether. The memory flashed in her mind as she began to shiver uncontrollably. She thought about her mother, laying in the bed cold and completely drained from all components of life.

Magnus handed her a tissue and waited for her to wipe away her tears and calm her thoughts. He picked up a black glossy glass box, and proceeded to open it. He pulled out a small gold crest that had the same images as the crest on the front gate of the house. "I would like to present you with this pin, and invite you back here in a week for the official induction ceremony on June nineteenth at 11:00 pm. When you arrive, you must show up wearing this pin," he said as he leaned in and stuck the pin on the top right breast area of the robe. "Joining the Illuminus Society will change your life."

"But what if my life doesn't need changing?" Elizabeth asked. "Well, you could decline our invitation and stay at the World and Trust Bank and continue to endure racism, sexism, misogyny, and the list goes on. Or you could accept our invitation and gain all the success, wealth, and advancement a person could hope for." Elizabeth glanced at the crest on her robe. She thought about how things had been going for her up until this point. "Wait a minute. How do you know all of that?" She asked. "It is my job to know," he said as he smiled and made his way towards the door "I hope to see you at the induction ceremony, Elizabeth. You deserve a better life. And, your mother would want you to be there," he said as he exited the room.

Elizabeth thought about his choice of words. Her mother would want her to have the best life. But, how could she be certain being inducted into a secret society could get her there. She had searched for answers for months on how to come out of the emotional rut she had been stuck in due to her mother's death, the stagnation of her career life, and the loneliness she had endured since Jonathan had gotten into a serious relationship and was no longer around that often. Elizabeth thought about the spirit she had seen upon her arrival.

Before she could think any more about the huge choice, she arose from the bottom of the tub and gasped for air. She was still dressed in the robe, and sitting in a tub filled with bubbles and Himalayan salt. She looked down to see if the pin was still in its place. The crest was still planted on the rob. It helped her to realize she was not dreaming.

Elizabeth had struggled for months to find herself. After dealing with one struggle after another and feeling plagued by the events taking place at her job, she had completely wiped away all memory of being able to project herself outside of her body after she was plagued with the death of her mother. She was unsure of what the Illuminus Society truly was or what it could do for her. But, after the night she had experienced, she began to think it was worth a try.

Elizabeth slipped on some dry clothing and curled up under her covers. She was alone in an unpredictable world with no one else to rely on but an uninterested cat, and her childhood best friend who had kept his distance at the request of his jealous fiancé. It couldn't hurt to see what the Illuminus Society was all about. After all, she had endured some hard days lately, and every hard working woman deserves success and happiness, she thought to herself as she pondered on what to do.

Magnus was convincing and he knew too much about her life for her to not dive into the world of the Illuminus and see what they could offer. In one night, they had helped her to find herself, revealed her gift of astral projection to her once more after she had deliberately blocked out her ability. Elizabeth placed the pin on her nightstand and prepared herself for sleep. She was determined to wake up tomorrow with a new attitude, drive, and ambition to get a new job after walking away from her position at the World and Trust Bank.

7

The Gifted

Giselle sat at her computer desk working on the loads of work that seemed to be compiling itself all around her. Running a business was not what she had expected it to be. She started to get a feel for the real complexities that took place when providing care for so many different types of people. She stared at her screen, and tried to conclude what made more sense; her Psych paper or her employee schedule? "So much to do in such a little duration of time", she thought quietly to herself as she looked over the list of available employees.

A text alert popped up on the screen of her phone, invading her efforts. "What's up Boss lady?" Giselle starred at the text. She attempted to consider the possibilities for who it could be. All of her employees were her programmed contacts, and a romantic relation-ship had never existed for her for the past few years. So, her list of who it could be was short-lived.

Giselle's intimate life was so bland and uninteresting to her that she started to consider the possibility that she was asexual. Her lack of interest in sexual intimacy was a bigger psychological problem than what she would have preferred for it to be. It didn't make sense to her constituents how someone as young, beautiful, and ambitious as she could be partnerless.

Surely, there was someone she was hiding in the shadows that awaited her texts and calls beckoning to slide through at any given moment and give her the attention she was lacking. But there was no one.

There were many suitors who watched and waited for an opportunity with Giselle. They often felt the sting of rejection when she declined an offer for dinner or a minute conversation. In the minds of her male admirers, who dreamed of getting a glimpse of who she was as a woman, she was deemed as uptight, bougie, and uninterested. Giselle didn't find any of the offers appealing.

Often, she clung to the excuse of having to work and study being her reason for the lack of companionship. Giselle never wanted to own or admit the fact that she was simply not interested for reasons that were deeply embedded in her subconscious. These reasons sparked the feeling of nausea anytime she thought of being physically intimate with anyone. Friends and family often concluded that Giselle's choice to remain a virgin was an unbelievable choice based on the visual imagery of what she looked like, and what she had. Often, hearing everyone reference her as being hypergamous when the actual reality was her anxiety towards sexual intimacy and the thought of partaking in it disgusted her based on all the stories she had heard from her friends who were currently being cheated on in their relationships.

Tamra made it a usual habit to try and set Giselle up with young men. She often felt slighted when Giselle would decline. How could she play matchmaker when she was failing at finding her own suitable match? Tamra held on to her insufficient relationship with Lamont despite his dire need to "matchmake" himself with other women in their community.

After wandering off in thought, she came back to the mysterious message. "Who is this?" Giselle texted in response to the bland text from the unrecognizable number. She waited for a reply as she continued to glance at her employee scheduler, filling in holes to make sure all of her clients were accounted for and paired with an adequate caregiver who could meet their needs properly.

"This Lamont," the text reply read. "Your cousin, Tamra, gave me your digits. I wanted to reach out to you to try to see if you could help my grams. She has been declining recently and struggling with remembering things. A few days ago, she suffered a burn after lighting the stove and forgetting that it was on. I wanted to know if I could hire one of your girls to go over there during the day to help her out."

Giselle took a long pause before replying to the unexpected request from Lamont. Business was moving and moving faster than what she could have ever anticipated. Giselle didn't feel as though she had the manpower to take on another client but she couldn't help but to feel like she had to urgently care for this woman.

She glanced at her screen once more and attempted to find a potential slot of availability where Lamont's grandmother could be implemented. There weren't many options. She texted Lamont back requesting a day for them to meet so she could learn more about his grandmother's specific needs.

Giselle finished plugging in her weekly caregiver schedule, and prepared to start her studying. Final exams were in a few days and she had failed to prepare herself adequately and needed to get caught up. She logged into her student portal and glanced at the list of assignments that were passed due. This was her last semester in her master's program, and the workload had been extremely heavy.

She started daydreaming about her future and felt overwhelmed when she thought about what would be required of her in a doctoral program. Giselle had barely kept her head above the water in the master's program. She often fell short, missed deadlines, and still managed to be a solid B student. Although it was working for her, she knew she was going to have to do a lot better after graduation.

Some days, she felt like running a business and being a student were too time-consuming and she needed to pick one. Other days, she felt like not doing both made her feel incomplete, and there was no way she could ever choose between the two. Giselle began looking over her teacher's comments about her writing. Her professor's critiques of her literary works were not the best. She exclaimed that although it seemed she had included some great content for the formulation of her paper, it appeared she had a deficit when it came to citing information properly. There was no way she could ever make it through a doctoral program and complete a dissertation with her inability to understand how to cite information in the correct format.

Giselle stared at the comments repeatedly for minutes, rereading the word deficit as if it were a knife to her throat. She focused on the term and felt offended. Sure, she had made a few citing errors here and there, but it was not enough, in her opinion, for her teacher to describe her shortcomings as a deficit. Giselle had experienced many situations with Professor Gregory that left her under the impression that she was not favored by the educator at all. Often reading her comments, emails, and picking up shady undertones in each paragraph where she felt it was obvious that her teacher did not care for her.

She had made her way through life picking up on people's emotions and behaviors. Giselle often found it extremely annoying that she did not possess the ability to withdraw from her gift of behavior analysis; meeting strangers, sensing their feelings, and interpreting their behavior immediately with or without adequate information about who they were and how they felt. This gift was the very thing that had inspired her to go into the psychology field. She prepared herself for a long-term educational journey that would get her one step closer to becoming a behavior analyst.

She began to sulk in her teacher's comments when she heard a loud knock at the door. She glanced up at the clock, wondering who it could be. Who could possibly be banging on the door at 10:30 pm? Giselle opened the door reluctantly, confused to find that there was no one there. She looked down at her feet, noticing a package, sitting in front of the welcome mat that lay in front of the door. Glancing around again, she monitored the entire perimeter of the house, still, there was no one in sight. She retrieved the package and reentered the house fast, feeling a surge of uncomfortability move through her body.

Being a loner and striving for growth and success, often left Giselle feeling that there was no need to switch things up and invite people into her circle of life. She didn't have many friends or acquaintances, and there was no one she was associated with that felt comfortable enough to show up at her home at odd hours of the night.

Giselle sat at the table, glancing at the package, debating if she should open it. She fixated her eyes on the unusual seal that sat in the middle of the package. She examined it closely, shaking the box vigorously. It was light, inconspicuous, and sealed with an interesting crest she had never seen before.

She stared at the crest closely. She wanted to figure out what company or organization the package could be from. Giselle pulled up a search engine on her laptop. She typed in bird, book, woman, and eye to see what organization would be revealed. Illuminus popped up immediately, sparking more intrigue from the curious twenty-something as she clicked the link leading her to the webpage for the secret society. She scanned through the website to get a complete understanding of what the Illuminus society was, and why someone would have sent her a package when there was an interception in her search efforts.

A video image centered in the middle of her screen began to play without her assistance. The video began informing her of what the Illuminus Society was and why she had been selected. Giselle sat staring at the screen in disbelief as she took in all of the information. Gifted? Her? There was no way she thought to herself. She struggled to make sense of it all. She thought back to the previous weeks, recalling the numerous times she felt like she had been followed or was being watched. It was all starting to make sense to her. She glanced at the package again. This time unable to fight against the urge to open it.

She began opening the package, revealing a small shiny black box and a note. Inside the box was a tiny pin in the shape of the crest that was sealed on the front of the package. She looked closer, noticing the same four images from the front of the miscellaneous delivery. The small card enclosed included a note informing her of the date and time of the Illuminus induction ceremony.

None of it made any sense to her. She had never heard of a secret society for African-Americans. Giselle had no clue what an organization like that would want with her. She was a small business owner and student. Surely, they couldn't possibly think she had anything to offer their society. She placed the package and its contents to the side as she glanced at the clock once more.

She looked around her living room. There was nothing that needed cleaning. She walked into the kitchen. There was nothing out of place, only able to notice the trash needed to be taken out. Giselle pulled the trash bag from the can, preparing to take it out when the bag ripped at the bottom. The rip dispersed the trash and foul-smelling liquid spilled all over the floor of the kitchen. "Give me a fucking break," she cried out frustratedly while observing the mess. She grabbed paper towels, cleaning supplies, and gloves and began cleaning the mess.

As she began to clean, she forgot about the strange package and invitation she had received. Giselle thought about all the unfinished work she still needed to complete. She focused on her to-do list like usual, fretted over her GPA, and tried her best to formulate a game plan in her mind that consisted of her getting everything completed before finals.

Giselle tossed the last item into the trash bag. She coated the floor with a cleaner and stroked it briskly with a mop. She began to choke from the potent cleaning products, so she immediately opened the windows in the kitchen. She heard a strange noise through the window. She froze in place as she tried to listen for the strange rummaging noises again. But, there was nothing.

It was getting late and she was long overdue for some rest. Surely, her mind had been playing tricks on her. She reached for the trash bag that lay on the floor filled with the foul-smelling rummage when she heard the noise again. Giselle ran to the kitchen door, opening it abruptly, reluctant to find no one in sight once more. She reached for the lid of the trash can, dropping the bag in quickly after hearing a noise in the wooded area adjacent to her house. "Hello," she said, as she looked around prepared to find that she was in the company of a deer or a raccoon, but there was no one.

Giselle turned to reenter her home when she was overcome by a strong but strange feeling. She could feel the presence of something or someone, but she did not know who or why. She froze in place, finding that she was unable to move. Her head started throbbing, submitting an aura she could not explain. She could sense the presence of multiple animals in the woods. Some hungry, some frightened, and some tired. She could also sense the presence of a human. She felt his emotions as if they were her own. She could feel he was eager, knowledgeable, and worried. Why he was worried she did not know. But, she knew he was watching her and had been for quite some time.

"Hellooo," she yelled out again, getting no response. She started to sense a new emotion from the presence in the woods. Giselle sensed excitement from the hidden being as she stood in her backyard unable to move. She dropped her head now battling the inability to speak as her body began to shake vigorously on one side sending her into a seizure. Before collapsing to the ground and becoming unconscious, Giselle opened her eyes, finding herself in the middle of a cornfield surrounded by thousands of tall stalks of corn.

She began walking through the cornfield, feeling the sting of the dry heat caress her face. She walked and walked unable to make contact with anyone or anything besides the sun and its rays. She reached the end of the cornfield covered in sweat. She approached a tiny rundown shack. There on the porch sat a man in a rocking chair. He rocked back and forth with a long wheat stalk hanging from his mouth. The man was dressed in dirty overalls, white long johns that appeared to be saturated in dirt, and a brown hat that covered his eyes and face from the sun due to the oversized brim of the hat.

Giselle looked around feeling confused. She tried to make sense of where she was and how it was she had arrived there. "I been waitin' for you," the man said in an old-time country accent that was unrecognizable to the well-spoken young girl. Giselle froze in place. "No need to be frightened. Surely an old man like me shouldn't scare you." "Who are you?" Giselle questioned, still standing frozen in place, waiting for the old-timer to explain to her how it was she had arrived there, and what it was he wanted.

"Well, if you get your scrawny behind up here on this porch and join me, I can give you the answers to all of that," the old man said as he continued to rock back and forth, chewing the wheat stalk. Giselle sat in the dusty rocking chair, awaiting the conversation with the old man who in her opinion seemed rude. "Scrawny? Who was he calling scrawny? Clearly, he was too old to understand the term slim thick or recognize it when he saw it," she thought as she awaited his explanation for her arrival. "I'm your kinfolk. My name is Cristophe, your ancestor." "Ancestor?" Giselle questioned. "What you can't hear? That's right, your ancestor. Pardon me if I seem a bit irritated. But, I've been sitting here for weeks watching and waiting every day hoping you'd show up." The man said in a snooty tone.

"I have been fighting off the urge to intervene. Cause, well, you was takin' too long. I started questioning if you was one of dem ones that got all the book sense with no common sense." "Wait a minute, who are you, and what are you talking about?" Giselle asked as she became annoyed with the man as he repeatedly insulted her while he rocked and rocked away in the dusty old rocking chair in the dry heat.

"Now, listen here. You wanna know something, I can tell you, but one thing we gone get straight is you better watch how you speak to me," he said earnestly, feeling offended by the clueless young girl. "I'm Christophe like I said earlier. I'm your kinfolk. Judging by your late arrival, it appears to me that you tapped into your gift. And, well, that's why you sitting here with me. Like I said, I've been waiting on you. Wondering if you was ever gonna get it figured out. You sitting around with your nose in dem books instead of tapping into your god-given purpose."

"What god-given purpose?" Giselle asked, still not sure what the grumpy old man was referring to. "You mean to tell me you done come all this way and still don't know nothing. You're here because you are gifted. In fact, you come from a long line of gifted people. Your ancestors were brought to America on slave ships. Many of them possessed strong abilities that were watered down or forgotten about after the rise of the slave culture."

He continued, "My mother, Sowar, who is your great, great, great grandmother possessed the ability to see things before all that took place. She also possessed the ability to conjure spirits from the past. The day we were taken into captivity, she warned me that men would be coming to take us and our lives would change forever. That day, she made me promise to remember my gifts. She told me they would try to make me forget. So, I made her a promise, that day, that I would not forget and I didn't. For years, I watched people lose hope and shortly after forget their gifts. So, I made it my duty to make sure people never forgot. Telling myself as soon as I was old enough, and strong enough I'd be a savior for my people."

Giselle sat in the rocking chair, swaying back and forth hanging on the old-timers every word. "So, what did you do?" she asked. "I started studyin' my own gifts closely. Learnin' what made them tick. Watchin' when my gifts would come fourth learnin' my triggers. I prayed to my ancestors, askin' for help, and one morning I woke up and I was told I was a free man. I traveled all over looking for people who could remember their gifts while helping those who could not, and in time things started to change."

"One day, I came across a man named Sam Brown who had been travelin' all over tryna recruit colored folk. He was tryna build up a society of blacks. Tryna help us get everything that had been stripped away from us, so he said. I joined him on his journey. The Illuminus Society is what he called it. Opening his doors to many, if not all of our ancestors. Givin' us a nice safe space to practice using our gifts and building our lives. Many of us had been living in fear for so long when Sam came about we was happy to have somewhere to go. A place to be where we could be accepted and we could live good. In return, all I had to do was act as a recruiter, showing myself every time one of my ancestors recognized their gift," the old man said as he continued to rock and chew on the wheat stalk. "Occasionally waitin' round for a dummy here and there to figure out they had a gift," he continued, glancing up at the offended young lady.

"I'll have you know I'm far from dumb," Giselle responded. "Yous a lie. How long it took you to get here? I thought maybe you was on the short bus. Ain't that what y'all like to say," the man asked as he began to laugh, still rocking in his chair aware that he had hit a nerve as he assessed Giselle's unamused demeanor.

"You ever wonder why you can meet somebody and get a feel for who and what they really are straight out the gate?" The old man asked. "I'm sorry, but I'm not following you," Giselle replied. "Yea, I know you not, short bus," the man responded under his breath. "Let me break this down for you so you can understand what it is I'm tryna tell you. What is it you wanna do with your life?" The old man asked to give Giselle the clue it was clear to him she did not have. "I want to be a behavior analyst," she replied, still uncertain where the old man was going with his line of questioning.

"You ever wonder why you so good at picking up on people's behaviors and emotions? Ever thought to yourself why that was? Women's intuition?" "I don't know," she replied with uncertainty. "Ever since I was a kid I have always had this extra feeling of intuitiveness. My grandmother always told me I acquired it from my mother. She said my mother always knew when a person was lying.

And, she knew how to get the truth out of them, no matter how hard they would try to fight against her. My mother died when I was about six, so I don't have a lot of memories of who she was. I know I've always been a good reader of people. I can take one look at a person and get a feel for their sincerity or ingenuine emotions. That's why I decided to pursue a career as a behavior analyst. I figured it would be a great fit for me.

Christophe continued rocking in his chair listening as Giselle described her gift unconsciously. Giselle rambled on and on about her ability to pick up on other people's emotions. She conveyed to Christophe how easy it was for her to observe, and accurately assess other individuals. The rocking chair took a halt in its repetitive motion. The old-timer looked up at Giselle pausing in the chewing of the wheat stalk. "You still confused about what it is you have inside you?" Before she could respond, she felt a surge of dizziness shoot through her body and became weak. Her vision began to blur, fading her out of one setting and shifting into another.

She tossed and turned, moving around on the small sofa before plummeting loudly to the floor. Giselle felt the dizziness invade her brain space as she tried to gain coherence. The pounding beat of confusion pressed up against her skull as she tried to understand what had happened. Her vision began to clear slowly as she watched a tall unfamiliar presence pull her from the floor, helping her onto the sofa. She opened her mouth to form a sentence, but the words would not emerge. She felt the fog, compiling in her head as she tried to make out the presence that was currently assisting her.

"Try to relax," the voice instructed, helping her to lie back onto the pillow while propping her feet at the opposing end of the sofa. Her vision, while still bleary, was starting to clear, outlining the tall man visible to her. "Who are you?" She asked in a drained tone recognizing how depleted she was. "That is not important right now. Try to relax," he instructed once more as he watched Giselle try to remove herself from the sofa. He pushed her back onto the pillow gently, attempting to create a feeling of solace for her. He caressed the sides of her face as he watched her doze off. He kneeled down, planting his body in a face-to-face position with Giselle as her eyes closed dozing off while he watched her rest.

Kyle stared at Giselle for minutes, fantasizing about what she was like. He pictured her awaking from her slumber delighted to find her long-lost twin brother at her side. He imagined them being inseparable. He thought to himself about what her dialect would consist of in a conversation amongst the two of them. He had been following her for weeks, after learning of her existence. He tracked her down with the help of a prominent private investigator, who was also a member of the Illuminus Society.

Kyle felt like a creeper, hiding in the shadows, stalking the only blood relative he knew of since the discovery of his adoption. Kyle had spent months doing research to find a blood relative. He tracked down one dead end after another, before learning of Giselle's existence. Kyle tapped Giselle's phone, intercepting all of her calls, hacked into her laptop, getting a glimpse of her day-to-day work responsibilities, and kept track of her schedule. This allowed him to show up to locations, view his sister from a distance, sit down at the local coffee shop, and watch Giselle as she worked on her laptop, scan her papers from his screen, watched as she worked, admiring her vocabulary and grammar skills. He had recognized which twin had inherited the bulk of intellect while in utero. So many times, he wanted to remove the magazine away from his face, and approach her table and give her the proper introduction.

He yearned to let her know they were siblings. He was dying to inquire if she too had special capabilities like he. Stalking her repetitively, during the week, before sensing that she was starting to feel like she was being followed. He would watch her pick up the pace, before evolving from a light sprint to a full-on run on her way to Tamra's apartment. Kyle hated stalking his sister as if he were some sort of predator and she was ignorant, easily accessible prey.

As she lay on the couch, he gazed at her, admiring her outer beauty. Kyle wondered to himself if that was a quality she had acquired from their birth mother. He wanted to awaken his long-lost sister, and tell her everything, from the beginning to the end, starting with what he had learned of her existence, their lineage, and her gift. But, he did not. He knew Giselle had been offered a spot in the Illuminus Society. So, for now, watching from a distance was his best option. Within a few days, she would be inducted, and he would start implementing his plan to formulate a relationship with her. He planned to build off of her ignorance before telling her who he was and what he wanted.

Kyle stared at Giselle once more, noticing a small bruise on the side of her head. He took his hand and raised it gently across the area softly while caressing her skin with warmth. He watched as the bruise withered away, disappearing as if it had never occurred. He placed a throw blanket over Giselle, tucking it under the sides of her body, feeling the honor of having had his first up-close look at the only real part of his biological lineage he knew existed. He wondered right away what it was that could have urged their mother to give them up.

He hated the idea of Giselle becoming a member of the Illuminus Society. During the duration of his time as a member, he was starting to take notice of many things that made him feel as though the society was in fact too good to be true. He thought about Silver, and how he was currently grooming him for a position he did not deserve or desire. He also thought about the level of arrogance and prestige Queen Mother possessed in her tone as she communicated with her inductees through a loudspeaker never giving them the option of knowing what she looked like or who she truly was.

This plagued all of them with questions and desires to know more about the assertive feminine voice that communicated instructions to all in the mansion over a loudspeaker never leaving the house unless she was in disguise. She covered herself in designer capes, scarves and shades. She exited the building to show up to the necessary meetings and events conveying her high fashion, desirable characteristics as she walked into rooms sprinkling her superiority all over the place.

Kyle had spent his days as a child drifting from one foster home to the next. Never knowing the comfort of real love or care. He dreamed of the day he would be old enough to exit the realms of poverty, abuse, and lack of comfort. He transformed himself from a troubled young boy to a successful eager young man, gallivanting through his late teens in search of one great opportunity after another. He never knew the blessing of longevity in any of his endeavors as he rotated between his desires of wanting better for his future. He was constantly in search of the answers from his past.

Kyle imagined what their mother was like. Did she have Giselle's eyes? His spirit of determination heightened, as he compared character traits between him and his newly found relative. He began looking around to get a feel for who Giselle might be from the things she had laid around her home. He noticed how organized she was, another shared characteristic between the two of them.

Kyle had been shuffled around and experienced many forms of abuse both physical and psychological. This forged a potent case of OCD that seemed to be prevalent in him and his sister. He wondered if Giselle had grown up in a good home. She certainly seemed to be doing well for herself. Maybe she was fortunate enough to be taken into a great home filled with love and care. The kind of love and care he had never been lucky enough to know.

Kyle made his way around the room still examining shelf after shelf, room to room. He took an abrupt pause after hearing the door handle rattle. He darted to the back of the house, planting himself inside the bathtub, hoping the shower curtain would serve as the perfect veil to keep him hidden from the unexpected guest. Footsteps roamed around in the background. Whispers amongst what sounded like two or more people. Why would someone be roaming around Giselle's home whispering? Kyle exited the bathtub slowly and quietly to remain hidden while peeping out the intruders. Making his way to the door, getting closer and closer, he heard a floorboard erupt making a loud creak.

"Is someone there?" A voice questioned, while the whispers continued in the background amongst the intruders. Kyle reached for his gun, barricading himself behind the bathroom door ready to defend himself if needed. The voices became faint, diminishing completely. Was Giselle in some sort of trouble he wondered as he clutched his gun still preparing for a potential attack. The door closed loudly, alerting Kyle that the intruders had made their exit. He heard a car engine start, sending him back into the living room. He peeked through the shutters to get a glimpse, watching as the all-black SUV sped away without any clear indication of who had been there moments earlier.

Giselle started to move around on the sofa. She appeared to be coming out of her slumber. Kyle knew he couldn't let her wake up and find him there. Him, the perfect stranger. What would he say? How could he explain to her in a reasonable way that he had been watching her for weeks, waiting to introduce himself properly? How would he explain how he so happened to be in her living room, staring down at her like some predator? There was no way she would understand or feel comfortable meeting him under such strange circumstances. He slid out of the back door without being spotted. He wanted to check on Giselle and make sure she was okay before parting, but he knew there was no logical way he could do so.

The induction ceremony was a few days away. Giselle had received her invitation and discovered her gift. So, for now, all he could do was play the waiting game. Wait for Giselle to make her choice. Once she became an inductee, his plan would be in motion. He could build a bond with his long-lost sister, and together they could track down their birth mother and learn more about their lineage. After all, what was the point of being gifted without knowing where your gift originated from?

Kyle prayed things would go as simple as he had been hoping. There was no way Giselle would learn about him, and their mother and not want to know more. He needed her to know more.

He drove away deep in thought, while his mind circled around the millions of unanswered questions that still remained unsolved. Giselle's gift seemed to be tremendously different from his own. There had to be a way to get to the bottom of their gifted origins, and Kyle was determined to figure out what that was.

8

The Mother of All Lies

Johnathan sat at his desk, waiting patiently for his new client to arrive. She had scheduled her initial visit for 10:00 a.m., and it was now 10:16. He hated the minutes that seemed to pass by slowly when awaiting the arrival of a new client. He wondered if she would be a no-show. He pictured her as a client who was building up the courage to overcome the anxiety that took over when contemplating a conversation with a stranger. A stranger who was responsible for listening to the good, bad, and the ugly with the main objective being understanding.

Johnathan felt like the world's biggest hypocrite. There he was sitting at his desk ready to help someone else understand their choices while he was failing to do so in his personal life. He tried to convince himself that he would prevail, acting as his own aide in his emotional internal saga of love and life.

Alicia had been good to him, offering him the many resources she had at her fingertips. This included the capital that initially got his business off the ground. Yet, he couldn't help but own up to the fact that he was not in love with her. How could he possibly commit to someone he felt no desire to build a future with? This was the million-dollar question he asked himself daily when he woke up to Alicia. He laid next to her tossing and turning while he fought off the urge to scream out the inevitable.

The clock was ticking and there was no way to avoid telling Alicia what he truly felt. He had talked with so many clients who were trapped in loveless marriages looking for an escape. They often found escapes through unconventional methods that ended badly. Johnathan couldn't deny his situation any longer. If he didn't do something soon, he would be one of those men that he didn't want to be.

He glanced at the clock once more, noting it was now 10:22 and there was still no client. He picked up the file on his desk. He began to take one last brief scan over it before calling the client to see if she had backed out. As he looked over her file, Karen Black walked into the building, dreading the encounter with the new doctor.

She had been to see many shrinks in the past. All they had managed to do was shrink her respect for the psychology profession as a whole. What could a stranger help her determine about her family's tragic murder other than the obvious? She was angry, hurt, and most importantly she wanted revenge. The obvious emotions were seeping through her pours daily with no intervention available to her. She had spent months roaming around Bali, after her abrupt encounter with the Illuminus Society, attempting to locate Gardega.

She feared the Illuminus invitation was an attempt made on behalf of her enemies. Someone had figured out she was on Gardega's trail and had warned him. But, that was not the case. Now, it was back to square one for Black. She didn't like the emotions that had been afflicting her since she had lost track of the criminal responsible for her family's murder.

Black sat in the waiting area deep in thoughts as she awaited the shrinks invitation. She hated elongated periods of time where she was required to sit with herself; sitting with all of the thoughts, emotions, and fears that were currently driving her life as she battled with what the next step would be for her. Most would have chosen normal methods to seek out healing; meditation, church, or time with loved ones. But, Black had a different plan in mind. She hated therapy. Visiting Johnathan's office and having normal sessions was all a part of her elaborate scheme to get to the next plot in her plan.

She had learned of Johnathan's existence from her old high school friend, Omari Bronson. Omari believed in Johnathan and his methods as a therapist. He felt Johnathan could be of assistance in her healing process. Karen was not convinced, but she reached out to Johnathan in hopes he could serve as a reliable piece in her long-drawn-out puzzle of corruption. As she put together a revenge fueled scheme to bring her family's killer to justice.

"Ms. Black, today's your lucky day," Johnathan said as he approached her with a smile on his face. "I usually don't see clients if they are more than twenty minutes late. However, my next appointment just canceled so you may come in," he said, leading her to the door.

"My name is Johnathan Meadows," he said while extending out his hand for Black to shake, but she did not. "Sorry, Doc. I'm a bit of a germaphobe," she said in an unbothered tone as she looked around the room assessing the well-organized office space. Johnathan smiled sitting in his seat, assessing Black while he watched her assess the room in depth.

"Good looking office space you got here," she said, holding strong to her nonchalant demeanor. Johnathan pulled out a fresh pocket-sized notepad, and wrote Karen's name at the top of the first sheet. "Why don't we get started? Tell me a little about yourself." "What would you like to know?" She asked. "Why don't we start with what brought you here today." This was it…the moment they all waited for, she thought to herself. She took a deep breath as she prepared to tell her story. Karen went into detail about her work life, family life, and her family's tragic death.

Johnathan stared at Black. He tried to understand her as she gave him bits and pieces of who she was and what she had gone through. She walked him through the tragic events of her family's death, making it clear to him the level of furry that ran through her veins each time she recanted the events that had ripped her world into shreds. Johnathan couldn't look past the hurt in Black's eyes as she conveyed to him the hole that was left in her heart.

Most who looked at her just saw an ambitious, aggressive, masculine form of a woman. But, he saw something else. Black was hurting and experiencing unimaginable pain. He picked up on her disdain for psych doctors as she hinted numerous times how she didn't feel a shrink could do anything for her situation. She made it blatantly clear that she was uninterested in healing, stating to him over and over that she felt there was no hope for her.

"How can I live with this type of pain? I've heard people say numerous times that you can never get over losing a child. I've lost my brother and two nieces. And, I now know what those people feel who have lost their children. Nightly, I suffer from insomnia, living with only two sleeping experiences. I am usually unable to sleep at all. That's why the bags under my eyes have their own bags. Or I am constantly awakened from what little sleep I can get due to night-mares."

"What kind of nightmares?" Johnathan asked, curious to see what demons dwelled in Karen's dreams, invading her comfort as she tried to put the day's pain to rest. "The dreams are always the same," she replied. "I walk into my brother's home, and I'm carrying bags." "What kind of bags?" Johnathan asked. "Gift bags, or maybe they are shopping bags… I don't know… They're just fucking bags. Okay." Karen replied in a snappy tone, frustrated with the good doctor for getting her to open up within minutes after conversing with him.

She wanted to open up, spill the beans, and move forward, but she wasn't sure why. Maybe it was Johnathan's calm, relaxing tone as he let his questions roll softly between his lips as he appeared to be calm, helpful, and interested in her pain. Maybe it was his handsome face, and lightly scented collar shirt that pressed up against his well-toned body structure. Or perhaps she was just tired. Tired of holding it all in, holding back, and letting her pain drive her. Tired of the pain that kept her stagnant and in a space of darkness she was starting to recognize too well.

Johnathan was not bothered by her curse words and snappy responses like some of the other psychiatrists she had seen in the past. It didn't bother him, because he knew she was a scorned woman, looking for a window of normality in a life that would never be the same again. Lashing out is a normal part of the healing process. So, he did what any good doctor would do and he apologized, nodding his head with a smile to give her a signal, letting her know she was welcome to continue with her description of the dream.

"Like I was saying. I walked in with bags for my nieces. I waited for them to run into my arms and greet me like they normally do. However, the house is silent and there is no one in sight. So, I start walking through the house calling to them and I get no response. I walk into their bedroom and I find them both…" Before she could finish the sentence, her voice started to crackle, making it clear to him that she was unable to proceed with the rest of her story.

Johnathan could tell from the look in Black's eyes that she was in distress. He did what he felt was right and proceeded to come to a close with their session, when they were interrupted. Johnathan got a text from the receptionist urging him to turn on the news right away. "Would you like some water? He asked as he watched Black struggle to pull herself together. "I'm fine," she replied, holding back the sniffles that were progressing against her will. "I think we can stop here for today, if you'd like. You seem a little upset." "It's ok. We can continue," she said, still holding her composure as she continued to suppress the tears that wanted to come flooding out.

"Something has been brought to my attention, and I'd like to check it out. Then we can pick up where we left off." Johnathan said as he turned on the television. He was shocked to find Omari's picture at the forefront of the screen. The news anchor stated that his body had been found in a parking lot of a deserted old construction site. It had been dismembered with his head plastered in the passenger's seat separated from the rest of his torso. The police also noted that his wallet, Rolex, and phone were missing.

Johnathan could not believe his ears or eyes. He tried to piece together what he was hearing when he looked over at Karen. He noticed the paleness of her skin tone as he assessed the shocked look on her face. Before he could form a sentence to inquire if she was ok, he watched as she darted out of her chair, fleeing away from the room instantly. "Karen, wait!" Johnathan screamed as he watched her run away without looking back. He followed her to the door, unable to calm her or get her to turn back and communicate to him what was going on. Johnathan was unclear about what had happened. But, it was obvious to him that Black had some sort of connection to Omari.

Johnathan returned to his desk, thinking about the shocking news report. There were so many things that did not sit well with him about the report. The news anchor had reported the crime as a potential robbery gone bad, but Johnathan did not agree. What kind of robber has the time or intent to cut off a man's head over a watch and wallet? Johnathan questioned as he sat in the chair shaken by the report.

He thought about his last conversation with Omari. He wondered if the revelation he was trying to reveal, during their last session, had something to do with his death. The phone rang, intercepting his thoughts. "Johnathan Meadows speaking." There was no response. "Hello," he said again, waiting for the breathing to cease on the other end. "Omari was not a victim of a robbery," the caller implied. Johnathan paused recognizing Black's voice.

"Is that why you ran out so fast? You knew Omari? Why do you believe it was not a robbery?" Johnathan was interested in hearing the distressed client's opinion. "I just have a feeling there's more to it," Black replied. "I'm afraid you may be right, it's unusual for a robber to decapitate a victim," Johnathan said as he thought more about the Illuminus Society, and what it could have been that Omari wanted to reveal to him.

"Do you know if Omari had any enemies, or knew of someone who may have wanted to harm him for any reason?" Johnathan asked. "He was a black wealthy athlete. I'm sure he had enemies," Black replied rudely, suggesting Johnathan's question was not a very good one. "Have you ever heard of the Illuminus Society?" Johnathan asked candidly as he tried to remain inconspicuous so there was no breach of confidentiality based on what little Omari had been able to share with him prior to his murder.

Black froze up on the other end, feeling startled by the question. She didn't know much about the secret society, but she knew the name itself sent chills up her spine. How was it that Johnathan knew of the existence of Illuminus? Was he one of them she wondered? She thought about the unexpected invitation she had received from the society during her time in Bali. Karen was a firm believer that if it sounded too good to be true it usually was. And, there was no doubt in her mind that the Illuminus Society was too good to be true.

Had Omari become tangled with Illuminus and gotten himself killed? Questions were roaming around in her mind back-to-back, leaving her completely zoned out while Johnathan continued. She tried to regain her attention on the other end of the phone. She had a hunch of her own and she was going to do what she could to get to the bottom of what happened to Omari.

Johnathan recognized that Karen was no longer actively listening. "Are you still there?" Johnathan asked. "I'm sorry. I got lost in my thoughts," she replied, still fixated on the proper angle to follow with the hunch that was brewing heavily as she took in the tragic event. "Maybe you could come in for a session on…" Before he could finish his sentence, he heard the dial tone beeping in his ear.

Black wasn't the first client to be put off by a tragic event to avoid the topic of therapy altogether. And, she most certainly wouldn't be the last. He thought about calling her back to convince her to schedule a session to talk about her thoughts on Omari's murder and whatever else she was feeling. But, he knew it would be a waste of time. He was unable to learn much about Black. However, from what little he had gathered from her, during their session, it was clear to him that she was a strong woman who didn't care for conventional mechanisms. He'd let her do what she felt was best for now, in hopes that when it was too much she'd do what most did, and reach out for a session.

Johnathan's phone rang again. He picked it up quickly, answering it hoping it was Black. "Well damn, I know it's been a minute, but you don't have to miss me like that," Elizabeth said, laughing on the other end while he said nothing in response. "I know my jokes aren't the best, but you could at least play along." "I'm sorry. But, I've had a crazy morning," He said, feeling disappointed that it was not Black's voice on the other end.

There was something about his new client that struck him as odd and intriguing. There was also a nudge that kept tugging at his intuition, telling him there was a lot more to Omari's story. "You ok?"

Elizabeth asked, after hearing the long drawn out silence from her distracted friend. "Why don't we meet up for lunch at the cafe in ten minutes. You can bring me up to speed with what's going on with you. I also want to talk to you about an opportunity I have been offered, and hear what you think about it."

Johnathan was not in the mood for croissants and conversation, but how could he say no to Elizabeth? Maybe he would feel better after sitting down with his close friend. He had been holding his feelings week after week. Maybe the time had come for him to tell her how he felt about her. Today could be the day he would finally have the talk with Alicia he had been avoiding for months. Every day, he entered a home he didn't want to be in. Every day he longed to exit his relationship, battling with how to do so properly without Alicia hating him. He didn't want to hurt her, but he was tired of hurting himself. Johnathan agreed to meet for lunch. He prepared himself to open up to his lifelong friend about his feelings.

He glanced at the clock and noticed two of the ten minutes he had left to meet Elizabeth had passed. He reached for the disinfectant spray, sanitizing the entire area. He grabbed the handheld vacuum, ran it over the top of his chair, the corners of the office, lastly vacuumed in between the cushions of the sofa he utilized for his clients only. The vacuum began to rattle loudly as if something had become caught in it.

Johnathan turned off the vacuum. He pulled it apart to see what the source of the loud clattering was. As he emptied the contents in the garbage can, he noticed something shimmering in the wastebasket beneath the dirt and debris. He reached for the shimmering item brushing around the dirt particles. He noticed a gold crest shaped pin and retrieved it from the debris. He held it up to the light to get a good look at the images. He focused on each image. He first glared at the woman, the bird, the eye, then the book. He wondered to whom the interesting looking pin could belong.

His phone chimed. Elizabeth had sent him a text with three eyeball emojis and a clock. That was her unique way of asking him where he was. He had become so engulfed with curiosity, after finding the pin, that he had forgotten about his lunch meeting with Elizabeth. "Headed your way now," he replied, sending her a thumbs up and a car emoji.

He placed the pin in his pocket, and grabbed his coat from the chair and raced to the door. Today was going to be the day he'd finally tell Elizabeth how he felt. He trusted that no matter what she felt in return he would have a huge weight lifted off his shoulders. He was certain Alicia would not take the news as well as Elizabeth would, but he could not go on deceiving her. There was no love in their relationship and he was ready to depart from all of the lies that had been tailgating behind him for quite some time.

Johnathan walked through the door of the cafe, feeling anxious as he mentally prepared himself for what he was about to do. He took notice of Elizabeth right away as she sat at the table, gazing out the window. Johnathan glared at her from a distance. He admired her entire existence. He looked at her plump supple lips, the dimples in her cheekbones, to the big bright eyes that were noticeable in any room she entered. There was something about her that seemed perfect to him. He loved how beautiful she was inside and out. He was drawn to the fact that, although she was gorgeous, she appeared to not have a clue of how beautiful her outward appearance was. His heart started to flutter as he moved closer to her table.

"About time you showed up. I asked the waiter to come join me instead," she said with a smile on her face. Johnathan's expression froze, unable to give Elizabeth any form of interaction in exchange for the sweet smile or witty personality he had grown so fond of over the years. "What's wrong with you?" She asked instantly, picking up on Johnathan's awkwardness. "I'm okay. I just had a strange day. Johnathan paused and noticed Elizabeth was wearing an unusual pin that appeared to be the same pin he had just found embedded in his sofa cushions.

Elizabeth kept talking unaware that he had become fixated on the crest pinned to the breast area of her blazer. "Hello!" she said loudly, breaking his focus. "Are you listening to anything I'm saying?" "I'm sorry. I got distracted," he replied. "The funniest thing happened to me before I left the office. I was cleaning the office and as I cleaned in between the sofa cushions…"

"Wait a minute," she said, interrupting. "You clean in between the sofa cushions at your office? I see why Alicia's desperately rushing to marry you. Do you have any free time available? I'd love to have you come over and give my place a tidying up," she said, laughing while her companion looked startled as he assessed her choice of words.

"What do you mean by that?" He asked in a bothersome tone. "By what?" Elizabeth replied, confused by his question. "What do you mean she is desperate to marry me?" He held an angry facial expression. "Chill, John. I was only making a joke. You know, hahaha. That thing we usually do when we get together.

Johnathan apologized, realizing he had taken the comment personally for his own reasons. Who was he kidding? She had a point and it was obvious to all. Alicia would have run down the aisle that very moment if he had extended the invitation. It was clear to everyone that she was in a rush. He couldn't help but wonder if it was clear to everyone that he was not.

"Anyway, what were you saying?" She asked as she changed the subject so her friend wouldn't feel embarrassed or bothered by taking offense when there was nothing to be offended by that she was aware of. "I'm cleaning and I hear this rattling in the vacuum. I found this interesting looking pin." "Ok, well what did the pin look like she asked?" "It looked just like the one you have attached to your blazer." She stopped. She had not planned on telling Johnathan all the details of the Illuminus Society and its offerings. But, he was her best friend. If there was anyone that was willing to keep her secrets it was him.

"I was offered a great opportunity recently," she continued. Johnathan noticed the look in her eyes as she went on. He glanced up at her with interest, immediately after hearing the urgency in her voice. "It's really kind of hard to explain but I...I," she said, struggling to find the words to express to her friend what she believed was the opportunity of a lifetime. "Take your time," he said eager for her to get it out and get it out in the proper manner.

"I was approached by an organization. A secret organization," she said with an ashamed look on her face. She feared he would either think she had lost her mind or she was being scammed. Optimism was not Johnathan's strong suit. "Hear me out," she said, alerting him that she was unprepared and uninterested in his oversight of what she had to say. "The organization is a secret organization for people of color. They help the oppressed, stressed, and the deserving find their place in this life by promoting and helping to shape people to become their best selves. They elevate them to a space of black excellence." "You sound like a spokesperson for them already," he said. Johnathan conveyed a false smile so she could feel comfortable enough to continue dishing out full details.

"They were aware of the things I had been going through at World and Trust Bank and came offering me a way out." "Had? What do you mean had?" He asked. "A lot has taken place since we last spoke, and well… I quit my job!" Elizabeth said with a smile on her face as if it were the best choice she had ever made in her life.

"Quit your job? Well, do you have another job lined up?" He asked in utter shock. "No, I don't," she replied, anticipating what he was going to say in response to her no. "Things were getting out of control there. And, after the last meeting, I had with everyone, it became clear to me that it was my time to go. "I understand your experience there was not the best."

"Not the best?" Elizabeth interjected, becoming instantly offended. "Not the best is an understatement. Every day, I walked into a work environment that was not designed for people like me, greeting an excess of uninterested faces, and getting no reply back. I held my tongue every time I had something to say in fear of losing my job for exercising my right to freedom of speech and freedom of thought."

"I curdled my ambition and intellect into a ball of non-discovery in hopes that it would allow others to respect me. I constantly told myself I would be safe as long as I hid the majority of my being, and packed it away in a mental storage compartment. I only allowed myself to come out to greet the sun when I exited the building for the day. I told myself that I, a young black woman, could rise and be great if and only if I hid my actual ability to be great. Make them feel as though I was not a threat and I would swim. Show them my capabilities and I would sink," she said as she started to get emotional.

"You don't know what it's like for me John. I lose no matter what I do. Do you want to know why that is?" She questioned, letting her emotions soar freely through the small, overcrowded café. "I am going to lose because I've chosen a lane that doesn't respect, acknowledge, or desire a black woman to excel or even have a seat at the table for that matter. What the fuck was I even thinking becoming a financial assistant, of all the things in the world I could have chosen."

Johnathan felt bad for Elizabeth. It was clear she was feeling something by his nonverbal responses so he tried to calm her down. "I'm sorry, Elizabeth. I never meant to offend you with my line of questioning. Tell me more about this society." Johnathan knew she must have reached her breaking point if she had decided to quit. Still, he felt like that was an abrupt choice despite the toxic work environment she had walked away from.

"I just worry about you sometimes, that's all. Ever since your mother passed you've been having a hard time. I just don't want you making rash decisions because you're overwhelmed. I can also admit the fact that I haven't been the best friend I can be to you in all of this, "Johnathan explained. He felt guilty as he recognized the pain and scorn present in Elizabeth's words.

He had been so wrapped up in his own life and issues he had never considered what daily emotional triggers could do to her self-esteem. In his opinion, she was strong, ambitious, honest and loving. Now, it was clear to him she had become someone else since her mother's passing. She had become vulnerable and discouraged, waiting at the gates of each day for support and resources she was not receiving. At that moment he wanted to suggest therapy, but he knew the current moment was not the best for the suggestion so he kept it to himself.

"Don't blame yourself for anything that's happening to me," she suggested. "Things have been rough, but I'm working my way through it. I left my job, yes. But, that was something that I should have done a long time ago. I've been offered a position in this society, the Illuminus Society. They have promised to change my life. All of my worries will be gone soon. The induction ceremony is a few days away, but after that things will change. I know they will," she said, sounding assured that this was a great window of opportunity for her despite her friend's questionable expressions.

"You said something a minute ago and I'm curious… You said the Illuminus Society is going to change your life and I was wondering how? Or rather how you could assume they are capable of doing so? Johnathan asked. Elizabeth looked at Johnathan. She felt anxious and annoyed with him and his spectator-like projections. Who was he to denounce what the Illuminus Society could and could not do for her?

"I know it sounds crazy, and maybe it is. But, right now I'm all out of options. My mother is dead, I am unemployed, and my best friend is getting married and isn't going to have time for me. So, you tell me, Dr. Meadows, since you seem to know so damn much. What should I do? Should I go back to the World and Trust Bank and beg for my job back? Or should I grovel back to my co-workers and play fake nice? Or maybe I'll go to the cemetery and dig up my mother's body and try my hand at a seance to bring her back? What do you think, Dr.?" She questioned in a pessimistic manner as she began to cry out loud not holding any of her emotions back.

"Judgy, judgy Johnathan…always dissecting other people's life and neglecting his own," she continued. "Maybe instead of worrying about me you should worry about why you are planning a wedding with a woman you don't even love," she said, wrapping up with one final insult as she prepared to flee from the table, her best friend, and the cafe.

Under normal circumstances, Johnathan would have chased her out the door, but he could not. Instead, he sat glued to his chair stunned by the read he had received that was right on point. Who was he to be judging her choices when he was currently making poor choices in his own life? He questioned whether Elizabeth had figured out his true feelings for Alicia based on the fact they had been friends for years, or if he was in denial at how obvious that component had become to the people around him. He couldn't help but wonder if Alicia too had noticed and did not care.

He sat at the table for ten minutes caught up in his own thought process, feeling like crap. Maybe Elizabeth was not wise to become entangled with this secret society, but who was he to judge her for that? She had no one and was desperate for some form of relief she had not known for some time. He thought about the many times he had rushed their conversations to make Alicia feel content, and how much the dynamic between him and Elizabeth had shifted to very limited contact.

Why had he neglected his friend for a woman he knew he did not want to be with. The answer was simple…he had become engulfed with the things Alicia was doing for him. He fell for the money, the lifestyle, and the networking resources she shared with him so fluidly. He never stopped to assess himself in time for honesty.

One of the main components Johnathan liked to highlight with his clients was the power of honesty and self-assessment. Yet, there he sat alone in the middle of a crowded cafe, experiencing the internal urge to flee from his own self-assessment. It had become painfully clear to him that he had allowed his desires for tangible things to force him into a relationship with a woman he saw nothing in. Alicia may have been many things, in the eyes of her constituents, but in Johnathan's eyes, she was bougie, self-entitled, privileged and suffocating. He couldn't relate to her no matter how hard he tried and that bothered him.

Elizabeth left in such a hurry she had no clue how the words she had spoken had left a scar. Although it pained him to be honest with himself, he knew the words that had parted from Elizabeth's lips were accurate. He did not love Alicia and it was time for him to be real with himself and his partner. Johnathan did know what would come of his life or lifestyle after he revealed what he needed to. The home they shared was a home Alicia had purchased. The car he drove was also under her legal ownership. He had taken the smart approach when building his practice so his business, building, and work-related items were all under his ownership although she had extended the funds to make it all happen.

Johnathan left the cafe determined today was the day he would approach Alicia with the truth. He was unsure of where that would leave him, but he had played a losing game for long enough.

Johnathan approached the large lavish home filled with nervous emotions. He noticed Alicia's mother, Betty Ann, parked in front of the home. Today was not a day he was prepared to deal with Alicia and her mother in the same environment. Johnathan entered the house, spoke to the women, avoided eye contact, interaction, wedding talk, and headed to his office.

As the women talked loudly about table settings, drapes, and seating arrangements, he could hear the excitement in both of their voices as they bounced ideas off one another. Johnathan tried to shut out the conversation, in the background, as he closed the door to his office. He hoped the barrier between him, the amber foundation, and the women would be solid enough that he did not have to be plagued with the sounds of their happiness. The happiness he had planned to strip them of when he came clean about his true feelings for the woman he was now certain he could not marry.

He sat at his desk and leaned back and forth in the reclining chair, gazing off into the abyss of emptiness. He stared off into space while his emotions unraveled internally, tugging at him with disappointment. How was it that he had become this disappointing shell of a man? How could he have waited so long? Why did he ask her to marry him in the first place? Was he truly so desperately shallow that he had allowed the resources she offered him to blindside him and lead him on a path he knew from the beginning he had no real desire to be on?

His phone chimed. "I'm sorry if I overreacted to your response today. I'm going through a lot and I need this one good thing! Illuminus may not be the answer to all of my problems, but I have to believe that it is better than the limbo I've been drowning in ever since the death of my mother. I just need my friend to understand and support me like I have always supported him…Sorry about the Alicia dig… That was low… and not like me. As Johnathan prepared a response, he noticed she was still typing. "I hope you can forgive and forget… you have Alicia...and I have… Well…Sprinkles, but she isn't that social. So, bare with me while I get all these icky emotions figured out."

Johnathan smiled and took notice of how he couldn't stay mad at her even if he wanted to. She had been very transparent with him. However, he had not reciprocated the same level of honesty. "No need to apologize," he replied "I became offended, but not because you were being offensive. I knew your comment about me and Alicia was accurate. No worries. You are going through a tough time, and I haven't been the best person or friend to you. You should never apologize for telling the truth… But, you should apologize for being mean," he replied in text. He followed his reply with laughing emojis and hearts to let Elizabeth know they were alright.

"I have decided today is the day I am going to let Alicia know how I truly feel. I'm calling off the wedding and the relationship. Just a heads up. I am most likely going to be homeless by the end of the night. So, I may need to come live on your couch for a few weeks," he stated in the text thread. "No worries…" She replied. "You're always welcomed on my couch…heart emoji.

Johnathan heard the front door shut. He raced from his office to the kitchen to see if the coast was clear, but it was not. There stood Alicia, sitting at the kitchen table on her laptop scrolling through images of bridesmaid gowns. "Where is Betty Ann?" Johnathan inquired. Alicia looked up with a soft smile on her face. "She'll be back. She went to pick up the cake samples. We're trying out some gourmet samples for the wedding."

Johnathan's face became red, alarming Alicia due to his dark brown skin tone. "John, are you ok? Do you feel sick?" She questioned, rushing to her feet and over towards the ashamed man, rubbing his forehead as if he were her sick child. Feeling concerned, he pushed her hand away, assuring her that he was okay. "I'm fine, but we need to talk," he said with a stern look on his face. "Okay," she replied, seating herself quickly after feeling alarmed by her partner's facial expression. There was something about Johnathan that did not seem normal to Alicia. However, she was unsure what the issue was. So she sat and prepared herself to listen.

"I really don't know how to tell you this but…but…I know I have to. I don't want to hurt you. I'm sure after I say this you will hate me, but it has to be said," he continued. "Tell me what? What's going on

John?" "I can't do this anymore," he said abruptly. "Do what?" She asked, still feeling confused by her partner's dialect. "The wedding?" Johnathan looked up at her, taking notice of the fear in her eyes as he prepared his response. "Not just the wedding," he stated in shame. "I can't do any of it...the wedding...the relationship...or pretending."

"What do you mean I'm confused." "I can't marry you because I don't love you," he stated bluntly, hoping to clear the confusion. "I don't understand. Did I do something?" Alicia asked. "No, you did not," Johnathan replied. "Is there someone else?" Alicia asked with a tremble in her voice. "No, there isn't," he replied. "Then why are you doing this? Why would you wait until a few weeks before the wedding to do this?" She asked with tears in her eyes. "I don't understand. How can a person just wake up one day and decide they are no longer in love?" She questioned him as the rage began to fill her heart that now felt as though it was sitting in her lap.

"I didn't just wake up and decide that I am not in love with you. The truth is I don't think I've ever been in love with you." Alicia's eyes opened wide with shock. "Are you fucking kidding me! She yelled out. The audacity she thought to herself. "Please let me finish, and then I will listen to whatever it is you have to say," Johnathan said in a calm tone. Alicia glared at Johnathan once more in disbelief.

"I realize I have been sailing through this relationship with wants. I wake up every day wanting to love you, wanting to be happy with you, and wanting to be content, but I am not. I also realize those things are not your fault they are my own. I made an initial commitment to you without truly knowing if that commitment was something I could see myself investing in fully. I've been committed, but I don't want to be. And, that has nothing to do with you. As I have said before, it's me. You are capable of receiving all the love in the world, because you are a wonderful woman. But, I'm afraid you're not the woman for me," he concluded.

Johnathan and Alicia heard a shuffle in the background breaking their attention away from one another to the back of the kitchen. There stood Betty Ann in complete silence and shock. She sat her bags down calmly, placing the box of cake samples onto the counter as she approached the discussion prepared to give her spill once the coast was clear. "I think I've overheard the majority of the conversation," she said in an unbothered tone. "You can continue," Alicia said while Johnathan sat in silence not uttering another word.

"Well, I'll finish since you're too much of a coward to continue in front of my mother. Good ole John has concluded today that he does not want to marry me. He also has had an epiphany and realized he is not in love with me," Alicia said as she made her way closer to the kitchen counter. "To add insult to injury, he has disclosed that in fact, he has never been in love with me. So, I guess you and daddy were right. He's just another piece of ghetto trash, looking to ride my coattails, and well congratulations to me for being a fool once again!"

Betty looked at Alicia as her eyes filled with tears. There she stood, feeling horrible that she had been right about Johnathan. From the beginning of the relationship, she could see that there was a lack of sincerity on behalf of Johnathan. Betty Ann had warned her daughter to tread lightly.

Alicia continued in a rage. "That's right. I said it. We can all see it. Good ole doctor John, the around-the-way boy with no money and no real options. Born and raised in a low-income community. Raised by a single mother…whom I happen to hate by the way. He had nothing... working a dead-end job and going to school. Then doctor John graduates and meets me, little miss unlovable. You wasted my time and my money, and used me for your personal gain."

"Alicia don't..." her mother interjected, but she continued. "Then you know what doctor John did next? He talked me into helping him build his practice with my family's money and resources, asked me to marry him, and then boom sits me down a few weeks before the wedding to tell me he is no longer interested. And the grammy award for best actor goes to doctor Johnathan Meadows!" Alicia screamed at the top of her lungs before smashing a cake sample in Johnathan's face, followed by another, and then another until the box of samples was empty.

Betty Ann grabbed Alicia, lunging her into a chair, urging her to calm down. Betty grabbed a dish towel drenching one half in water and leaving the opposing side dry. She handed the towel to Johnathan to clean the cake debris that was currently taking over his entire face. "I understand you are upset Alicia, but you have to be honest with yourself. You had to have seen this coming because your father and I did," said Betty.

Johnathan kept his head down as he continued, wiping the cake debris from his face. Alicia looked up alarmed by her mother's statement. "So, are you saying this is my fault?" She asked. "No, but you have to take accountability. No woman deserves to be hurt in this way. However, you had to have seen what he was about, because we all saw. In the beginning, he was so chipper, happy, and romantic. He stopped by and dropped off candy and flowers, appearing to be just as eager as you were to fall in love. I remember giving you a close observation one day when you stopped by to bring her one of your surprise pop-up gifts. I remember thinking to myself there goes a man that wants something. There goes a man who like most can spot a perfect opportunity when it's dangling in his face innocently."

"Are you implying that this is my fault?" Asked Alicia. "No, but I do feel like you need to be honest with yourself. This man did everything he could, in the beginning, to get and keep your attention and we all saw it. Once you started helping him and providing things for him that he couldn't provide for himself, that all changed. Your father and I could see all of this coming. Every time I stopped by to go over wedding arrangements with you, I would notice a change. John was not talkative as usual; running in and out as fast as he could as if he was trying to tell us without having to really tell us that he wasn't interested in a wedding. We all knew this wasn't going to last. But, we figured you'd get through at least a year or two of marriage before all of this took place. I understand your hurt, but you should be thankful God spared you some extensive heartache," Betty concluded, taking notice of Johnathan's silence and shameful demeanor.

"So, let me get this right. You're not implying that it's my fault, but you do think I should have been able to see it coming. I should have been able to see that the man I was loving and believing in didn't love and believe in me," Alicia recanted as she began to sob uncontrollably. While her mother caressed her head softly as she watched her unravel. "Is there anything you'd like to say John?" Betty asked, noticing how he sat silently while removing the leftover cake debris from his beard.

"Miss Betty please understand and believe me when I say I never wanted to hurt your daughter. She is a great person, but she deserves someone better and someone dedicated as we all know I have not been. I've wanted to be, but I can't. I don't want to spend another month or year waiting for those feelings to change, because I realize they won't.

"When did you realize this John? Was it after you had stolen my daughter's heart? Or was it after we helped finance your business? Gotten you an upscale client list? Or was it after you realized we all had invested so much into helping you become a better man." Betty Ann said with a sharp tone of sarcasm. "It's not like that," Johnathan interrupted. "It's exactly like that!" Betty screamed in an enraged tone.

Alicia looked up at her mother surprised to hear her so upset after misinterpreting her feedback surrounding the situation. "You came into our lives pretending to love and care for our daughter. We showed you love, respect, and care, looked out for you every step of the way. Not because we wanted to or because we had to, but because our daughter saw something in you. I told my husband many times that this would end badly. I could see it from the start. You came into this relationship with nothing but aspirations, dreams, and needs...all of which my daughter helped you to satisfy. The nerve of you to say it isn't like that. Son, it is exactly like that. Whether you choose to admit to it or not."

Johnathan knew she was right. It was indeed exactly as she had stated, and he knew he could not argue with Betty's wisdom concerning who he had been to her daughter. He had taken and taken until there was nothing left to take. Like most relationships that were built upon false pretenses, Johnathan was no longer interested, because the investments had run out.

He had no desire to admit to himself that he had used someone for his personal gain. However, the truth was the truth. He didn't love Alicia, and he never had. He had fallen in love with the resources he had access to and trained himself to believe he had fallen in love with the person providing them. Even when it had become clear to the people around him that he was uninterested in Alicia.

"I think it's best if I get my things and go," Johnathan stated, realizing he had no rebuttals or arguments that were valid against Alicia and her mother's claims of who he was. He had somehow envisioned things going a little different in his mind. He went to the closet they shared, and started grabbing his things preparing to pack them and go, but he was interrupted. "If you think for one minute you're going to leave here with things I've purchased, doctor, then you're sadly mistaken."

Alicia always referred to Johnathan as Doctor when she was upset. It had always been her condescending way of mocking his title. It was as if she was wanted to imply she didn't feel as though he had earned it despite his GPA and degrees that offered full proof that the title was earned honestly.

"Before I go any further, just what exactly will you allow me to take?" He questioned. He feared he already knew the answer. "You can take whatever you purchased with your own money. We'll look around. That's just about…nothing here."

Johnathan grabbed his work bag, laptop, and car keys and headed for the door. He was not in the position to fight with Alicia on any-thing. She was hurt and he knew she had every right to be. There was no way he could expect her to reconcile with him, or his request after waiting so long to end things with her properly. He exited the door prepared to hop in his car and leave when Alicia stopped him in his tracks. She abruptly reminded him that the luxury vehicle he was prepared to leave in was in her name, and would not be leaving the property.

Johnathan hung his head low, and felt the feeling of frustration creeping upon his being. Who was he kidding? Alicia had always been pretentious and petty and he had been a fool to think she would handle things any other way.

He stood in the middle of the cobblestone driveway frustrated that he was officially homeless and carless after coming clean with Alicia. He requested an Uber as he tuned out the countless insults Alicia was spewing out at him in the background. His phone alerted him that a small black smart car would be arriving in three minutes. Three more minutes of hell, he thought to himself as he stood in place mute, taking all of the insults that were casually being thrown at him by his bitter hurt ex-fiancé.

Alicia continued to stand outside taunting Johnathan with her negative digs as he waited for three minutes that seemed to pass by slowly. Elizabeth had assured him a few hours ago that her couch was his if and when he ever needed it. He knew she was going to be shocked that he needed it so suddenly, but that was his only option.

An black smart car turned the corner and entered the driveway slowly as Johnathan began walking towards the vehicle. He was desperate to get away from the scorned women he was no longer going to marry. He hopped into the Uber, feeling embarrassed as the Uber driver set her focus on the woman consistently yelling insults at him while she watched the car exit the driveway.

"Well, she looks pissed," the woman stated with a smirk on her face, as she drove the Uber. She wondered what Johnathan could have done to infuriate the visibly upset woman. "Break up, I'm guessing." "Yes," Johnathan replied sharply as he gazed out the window in hopes to avoid any more conversation with the young woman driver. "Relationships can be hard. I recently got out of a relationship myself," she stated while he continued to gaze out of the dirty Uber window. He overlooked the debris that clung to the window as he tried to think of what to say to Elizabeth upon his arrival.

"What did you do?" The driver asked. Johnathan took a deep breath before replying. "I called off our wedding that was scheduled to take place two weeks from now." The driver's eyes became big and dilated,
flooded with questions. "That was a bold move! What made you do that?" "I just felt like we weren't right for one another." "Well, you got to do what you got to do!" The driver replied in the hope to make him feel like less of a scumbag

"It's life! Sometimes, we feel like we do and other times we feel like we don't. So, kudos to you for being honest with her. She'll thank you one day!" "I highly doubt it," he replied. He was certain Alicia would spend the rest of her days hating him and standing firmly on that hate no matter what.

"I'm Mia, by the way. Mia Gonzales." "My name is Johnathan,

Doctor Johnathan Meadows," he said, still looking out the window. "Ooh, a doctor? What kind of doctor?" Mia asked. "I'm a Psychiatrist, "he replied. Mia laughed right away. "What's so funny?" Johnathan asked, confused by the humor she found in his response. "Nothing. It's just your a therapist, so I'd imagine you help people with relationship problems all the time. But, from the looks of things, you may need some help of your own. Kind of a cliché," she said, still smirking. "I guess you're right," he replied. He held a smirk of his own as he assessed the obvious irony

"Well, Doctor Meadows, we have arrived," said Mia as she pulled into Elizabeth's driveway. She took notice of Elizabeth who was exiting her car and was stunned to see Johnathan at her home without a warning text or call. "Well, Doc, it looks like you are big pimpin'. Well, what do you know, the irony," she said as she turned up the radio. The music played in the background. "I'm on to the next, on to the next..." she sang along with the radio, loudly sparking up laughter in the backseat.

"Well, would you look at that," she said with laughter to brighten Johnathan's day. "It's not like that. She's my best friend," he said. He had taken notice of what Mia was implying. "Well, Doctor Meadows, if I had a best friend that looked like that, I don't think I'd let some bougie financé get me down," she replied, extending a wink to the backseat as she watched him exit. "Take my card and reach out if you ever need a ride," she said as she handed him the card and turned up the radio as she pulled away from the home.

"Who was that?" Elizabeth asked as Johnathan approached her. He looked as if he had just departed from a funeral. "That was Mia, the Uber driver." "And why are you riding around in an Uber instead of your car?" "It's a long story. But, I'll give you the short version. I came clean with Alicia, and told her I was not in love with her. I called off the wedding. Within minutes, I became homeless and without a vehicle. The car was in her name," he said.

He looked so pitiful as he waited for her to respond to his soap opera drama. "And, you're here because?" she waited while he tried to find the words, but he could not. "I'm kidding, John. Come on in. You're welcome to stay as long as you like. Especially if you're going to engage in your favorite pastime vacuuming in between the sofa cushions for me," she said with a smile.

Johnathan grabbed the grocery bags from Elizabeth's arms and clutched his work bag tightly, praying he didn't drop it tarnishing his laptop. Elizabeth opened the door to her home, that in the present moment smelled of cat urine and stuffiness. "I'm sorry about the smell. Sprinkles likes to dabble in the occasional freelance urination practice when she feels like it. She marks her territory on my newly purchased decorative pillows." Johnathan glanced at the sofa.

He was uninterested in it being his place of resting. The thought of the cat's urine that could potentially be hidden within the linen made him feel nauseated. "Is this where I'll be sleeping?" He asked rhetorically. "It's not the Ritz, but I can trash the pillows and clean the cushions," she said. She was well aware that Johnathan's OCD had set in after giving her sofa one glance.

"What's for dinner?" He asked to change the subject. He wanted to take his mind off of the cat urine that had become embedded in his nostrils as soon as he entered the living room. "Vegan chicken and pasta," Elizabeth replied as she began unpacking the grocery bags. "Doesn't sound that appetizing, but us beggars can't be choosers," said Johnathan.

His phone went off, alerting him of multiple text messages he had received since his departure from his home and relationship. Before he could turn his phone off another text message came through. "Wait! Is this really happening? Did you really break things off with Alicia? You told her you don't love her. I've seen you with her. The two of you together are the epitome of black love in my book. This has got to be the mother of all lies. #coldfeetisnormal"

Johnathan read the text out loud, shaking his head at every line. "Who sent that? One of Alicia's clueless friends who wouldn't know black love if it hit him in the face, Mr. Divorced four times." "Four times? Maybe you two did look like black love to him!" Elizabeth replied in a sarcastic tone. "Relationships are funny like that. Outsiders always focus on the glitz and glamour of what they think a situation is, and then they become surprised and upset when they find out the truth." Elizabeth said. "Don't let that get you down. You did what you felt was best for the both of you. No one is going to understand that," assured Elizabeth.

She hated seeing Johnathan in this position. His phone continued to go off with text message after text message. Some from friends, clients, family members, and some from Alicia herself. Alicia had made it her business, within the thirty minutes of Johnathan being gone, to call and tell everyone she could about their breakup. "Neal doesn't know a thing about who Alicia is. How does he think he can text me talking out the side of his neck? The mother of all lies…the mother of all lies was the relationship itself," Johnathan concluded.

Elizabeth understood his frustration, she hated the idea of his clients knowing what was going on in his personal life. After all who wants a therapist helping them with relationship issues who has relationship issues. Alicia had always been calculated and low-key shady in Elizabeth's opinion. How was it that Johnathan was so surprised? He had stood by on the sidelines for years and watched her engage in shady deals and revenge plots against lifelong friends when she didn't get her way, Elizabeth thought to herself. The mother of all lies was him thinking Alicia would spare him the ugliness she dished out to others so freely.

The truth was Johnathan had spent the past few years taking resources from a mean rich girl who was not equipped to handle anything the way a normal adult would. Elizabeth didn't want to admit to him that she saw this coming, but she did. The mother of all lies was that her best friend had become shallow and sucked in by money, status, and abundance so badly he was about to risk his future for a future he never really wanted for the right reasons.

9

The Crest of Abundance

Giselle woke up dizzy and confused. Her head was throbbing, and her stomach felt nauseated. She could feel the urge to vomit piling up in her gut. Instantly, she guzzled down an eight-ounce bottle of water that had been left out overnight to suppress the sensation. She hoped hydration would be the answer to her problems.

She had slept the entire night away on her uncomfortable sofa which left her with back pain. She also woke up with confusion to find a box, a crest, and an invitation to a secret society she thought was nothing more than a dream laid out on the table waiting to be explored. She picked up the crest, twirling it around in her hand. Giselle was hoping to make sense of her invitation. How did the Illuminus Society find her? And what could they possibly want from her?

The nausea started to creep in again and sent her to the bathroom in a hurry. Giselle fell to her knees projectile vomiting all over the brim of the toilet. "Remember your gifts," she heard a voice say, roaming in the background. She looked around the room, but there was no one there. Great, I'm hallucinating, she thought to herself as she continued to kneel slumped over the toilet, waiting for the second round of vomit to emerge.

The room felt as if it were spinning, and she could not control the vomiting sensation that had taken over her morning. An image popped into her mind as she remembered the man from her dream. "Christophe," she said out loud. She tried to distinguish if it was indeed a dream or just a figment of her imagination. She had been working so hard lately, and ignoring the burnout she felt from her overload of responsibilities. It was clear she had finally cracked. Giselle leaned over the brim of the toilet, expelling out vomit once more. She didn't know what was going on, but she felt terrible.

Her phone began to ring. However, she was in no condition to answer. There she sat slumped over a bacteria infested toilet seat feeling drained and depleted in a way she had never experienced.

The nausea finally suppressed, leaving Giselle depleted with no one to care for her. She washed her face and brushed away the debris that lay embedded in between her cheek and gums. Back to the sofa she went, plopping down, covering herself with a duvet and a cold washcloth across her forehead. Today was the day she was required to complete her final exams. She was in no condition to do anything outside of laying on the sofa.

Her phone rang again. She did not answer. Minutes later she received a voicemail notification. Giselle ignored the notification as she lay on the sofa dozing off into a deep sleep. She opened her eyes surprised to find herself back in the company of Christophe on the old dusty porch. There he sat still rocking in his chair, chewing on a wheat stalk. "Back so soon," the old-timer said as he rocked solemnly in his chair.

"What am I doing here again?" Questioned Giselle. "You don't have to sound so excited," the old man said sarcastically. "I summoned you here. The Illuminus Society is going to be making its offers to all its new members today." "What does that have to do with me?" She asked. "I'm not a member yet." "Let me explain something to you so we can move this all right along. You don't choose Illuminus, it chooses you. You also are not at liberty to decline. And, if you do, you won't be a member of anything," the old man warned.

"Illuminus is connected, intricate and powerful. Once they set their sites on you, there is no going back. That's why I summoned you here to warn and prepare you. Once you have received your invitation the next step is the offering." "I don't understand...are you implying that I can't have a choice in the matter of being inducted? Are you telling me I have to do this?" Giselle questioned him.

"You don't have to do anything. But, if you want to stay alive, then, yes, I'm telling you this is something you have to do. As I told you before, all of your ancestors were a part of the society and you will be too." "What is this offering supposed to be?" Asked Giselle. She sat feeling even more confused than she had during her prior visit with the old man. "The offering is a financial blessing the Illuminus Society offers all of its inductees. This financial offering is based on a trade and comes with a price. After receiving it, you will be responsible to commit an act." "What kind of act?" She asked hastily. "It will be an act that will most likely displeasure you and cause you someone close to you. Once this act is committed there will be a severance of a relationship you hold dear. This will be the first exchange you will have to undergo during the induction process."

"I don't understand. Why would I willingly want to do that?" She asked as she tried to follow the old man and make sense of the information he was laying on her. "Everything comes with a price. This is the price that has to be made for all that you will acquire once you are officially inducted into the society. Your life is going to change in ways you can't even imagine. Illuminus requires this exchange as leverage and confirmation that you are completely invested in their mission to excel the black community. To whom much is given much is required. And, they will require many things from you. If for some reason you were to decline they will kill you. Within the first week, after your induction, your life will become something that is so perfect you will feel like your dreamin'. All that runnin' around you been doin' is gonna be put to an end, and you will never be worn out again," the old man assured.

"The society is gonna bring you much good, but it will also require that you earn it through tasks they feel only you can complete." "Why are you telling me all this?" Giselle asked, feeling like there was more to the old-timers prep sessions than what he had originally let on. "I need you to get in and find answers that I and others in our linage have been searching for for a long time, and came up empty."

"Answers to what?" Giselle asked, fearing what Christophe's response would be. "Your ancestors were all members of the society, as I told you. But, some of them didn't have a good experience. For years, Sam Brown ran the Illuminus Society and our people were happy. Sam taught us how to be excellent in ways we had never been shown before. Teaching us how to read, write, and be innovative."

"Before we knew it, we looked up and the small town we had created became a larger community filled with small towns of black folk, learning, and blossoming into greatness together. One day, some good ole boys came galloping through our small community on their horses. What they saw blew their minds and filled their lungs with hatred. Everywhere they looked there were black folks blossoming, and living better than any blacks they had ever come across. The leader of the group of white men was a man named Vincent Townsend. Townsend was a wealthy entrepreneur that was traveling through the south on business. I will never forget the look on those white men's faces when they came riding through Sparrow Grove."

"Sparrow Grove?" she asked. "That was the name of the first community in Virginia that Brown had put together before relocating to Georgia. We all lived there for five years before those white men came and ruined everything. Vincent took one look at what we had cultivated and we all felt the ominous energy risin' in the air. It was like looking a demon in the face before he sucked out your soul. That night, after the white men had traveled through our town, I had a dream. In the dream, your grandmother, Sowar, came to me warning me that the white men would be back and they would destroy everything we had built. I went to Sam and told him of my dream and he wouldn't listen."

"Later, the next day, a psychic who was new to the Sparrow Grove community came to Sam and told him she felt a great evil arriving whose aim was to tear down everything we had established." "So, what happened next?" Giselle asked, hanging on the man's every word. "We prepared for the attack. That day, Sam had us all gather what little we could to bring with us and we hid in the woods, waiting for the men to come and attack our community. A young lady named Suki, who we all referred to as Bubble, was the answer to our prayers that day. Those white men came trolloping through Sparrow Grove like they had received orders from the devil himself."

"They knocked down everything in their way and set fire to the entire community. We all hid in the woods and watched as they set fire to everything we had once owned and built with our hands. Bubble kept us protected, hiding us with her power to mask us away under her invisibility bubble, shielding us all from sight. We watched as they tore apart the entire community. They left nothing untouched or untarnished."

"We thought we had managed to get everyone out of there when we watched Townsend pull away one of the youngins who had somehow been left behind. The boy's name was Emmanuel. He had psychic abilities, just like you." Giselle paused, feeling thrown off by Christophe's comment. Up until that moment, it had remained unclear to her just what her gifted ability consisted of. She tried to act un-alarmed listening for the old man to finish the rest of the story she was finding to be interesting.

"Townsend kidnapped Emanuel, that day, and we never saw him again. We looked, prayed, and we even tried conjuring spirits to ask for guidance and help. But, we were never successful in locating the boy. We never knew what became of the boy. We all figured he was killed and tried our best to move on with our lives."

"After that day, Sam led us all to a new place where we rebuilt our community from the ground up. Within three months, we had a new community, and things were prospering for us all as it had before. Sam decided it was best if we remained hidden from the rest of the world out of fear that Townsend, or men like him, would come and tear us down again. That's when we all started praying to our ancestors regularly asking for their help. The spirits of our ancestors responded by showing us the old ways, and teaching us the things we did not know." Christophe thought it best to leave out that he had been appointed one of the leading spirit ancestors.

"Before you knew it, we were all stronger and our magic was stronger. We had Bubbles and all of the others like her use magic to shield our community from eyesight. Many a-times strangers like Townsend, settlers, and Native Americans would come breezing through our land never noticing we were there. For a long time, we lived in peace and continued to prosper. But, things changed when the Queen Mother took over."

"I don't understand. Who is the Queen Mother? Giselle asked. "She is the new leader of the Illuminus Society. You will never have an opportunity to see her face to face. She is the person who makes all of the decisions, including selecting the gifted inductees. She is at the top of the pyramid and calls all the shots. Once you are inducted you will forever be under the eye of the Illuminus Society. They will know where you go, when you go, and they will set perimeters around what you can and can't do. The number one rule you must remember to follow at all times is to keep the secret society a secret. If for some reason you were to break that rule, they would kill you," the old man warned.

"As I told you before, things in the Illuminus Society are no longer as they were. Sam was about building the weak, helping the poor, and cultivating togetherness. After he passed on, all that seemed to change." "What do you want me to do?" Giselle asked fearful of what Christophe's reply would be. "We will get to that when the time is right," the old man replied."For now, I just want you to prepare for the offering."

"Remember, the offering will bring you a financial reward. You will be gifted the reward in exchange for an inappropriate act that will ruin a relationship with someone close to you. You will want to decline, but you must go through with it to be inducted into the society. "What if it's something I really don't feel comfortable doing?" She questioned. Before she could get a response, she woke up back in her home on her sofa.

The offering sounded like the epitome of a catch twenty-two in Giselle's opinion. Why would she ever want to hurt someone important to her? There were so many possibilities in her mind. She didn't know what to think, but one thing was clear to her, declining the invitation was not an option. Christophe had made it clear that she had no other options outside of accepting. So, accepting the invitation was what she planned to do.

Her phone went off interrupting her thoughts. It was Lamont. He had inquired about care for his grandmother, and Giselle promised to reach out to him and didn't. "Shit," she cried out loud. There it was, another potential client she had forgotten to reach out to due to the burnout she was in denial about; lack of sleep and structure was starting to overwhelm her. She didn't want to take on Lamont's grandmother, but she had too many financial obligations to turn down a client.

Giselle texted Lamont back, apologizing for the delay. She scheduled a meeting with him. She needed something to distract her from her Illuminus worries and life altogether. "See you in two hours," he replied. Giselle pulled up her calendar on her cell. She searched her employee roster to see if there were any possible options for a potential caregiver for Lamont's grandmother. She glanced from name to name and saw no availability.

She had not worked as a caregiver in two years. Since the rise of her business, she had managed to be on the delegating side of things never having to work in the field with clients. She kept her job responsibilities to conducting client interviews, signing contracts, and pairing families with the right caregiver. She needed the money, but she didn't have an available caregiver so she decided she would do it herself.

Giselle still felt a little dizzy and uncertain of her future, after her last meeting with the old-timer she was learning to trust. She couldn't believe the turn her life was taking after learning she was a psychic. She had never done anything remotely psychic. In her opinion, she was more so intuitive than anything else. She didn't know what to make of Christophe's accusations about the Illuminus Society. Nevertheless, she was also not foolish enough to go against anything he said. If what he told her was true, she knew she didn't have any other choice in the matter, but to move forward with the induction process.

Giselle changed clothes and ordered an Uber. She prepared to meet up with Lamont and go over his grandmother's needs. Minutes later, a black smart car arrived and she hopped in. "Where would you like to go?" The Uber driver asked. "I know you entered it in the app, but I always like to double-check. I've had too many clients hop in, intoxicated and upset after I drop them off at the wrong address that they entered before I arrived," she said with a smirk on her face.

"You can drop me off at the vegan spot on Preston Avenue," Giselle replied. "Are you vegan?" Asked Mia. "No, but I am trying to make the transition. I work a lot and I feel really sluggish most days. Consuming mostly fruits and veggies gives me the energy boost I need to not feel like a zombie seven days a week," replied Giselle. Mia pulled up to the front of the restaurant when her attention was taken over by a young man dressed in designer garments standing in front of a luxury vehicle.

"Well, well, well, if it isn't Lamont sneaky ass," she said rolling her eyes. Giselle froze, fearing she was about to be told some information she wouldn't want to hear. She acted uninterested in the Uber driver's comment. Mia glanced at Giselle through her rearview mirror. "You got a man?" She asked. "No," Giselle replied. "I'm happily single and focused on my bag." "I know that's right," Mia responded. "You see that guy walking into the restaurant right there? We had been talking for a while. I thought we were dating until a few days ago when I found out he has a girl. It took me by surprise because he was always with me. Some dummy she must be," Mia said, shaking her head.

"That dummy you're referring to is my cousin," Giselle replied in an aggressive tone. "It's a small world," Mia said, looking embarrassed right away after hearing the irritation in Giselle's tone. "I'm sorry if I offended you. I didn't mean anything by it," said Mia. Giselle ignored

Mia's attempt to apologize, exiting the vehicle while removing the tip from the app before fully processing her payment.

She had heard many stories about Lamont's unfaithful behavior in regard to his relationship with her cousin Tamra. What the Uber driver had told her did not come as a shock, but it made her feel uncomfortable. She was not prepared to sit down and do business with mixed feelings about her client. She had to remind herself that business was not personal. For now, she needed to view Lamont with the same perspective as she would a client, whom she did not have any relationship with outside of work.

She entered the restaurant with a poker face on, greeted him with respect, although she felt as though there was nothing respectable about him. "What's up beautiful," he said, greeting her with a slick smirk on his face as he licked his lips. He stood up from the table, and pulled out her chair like a perfect gentleman. "Hello, Lamont," Giselle replied. She wanted to convey to him that she had no interest in his gentleman-like approach.

She pulled out a folder, pen, and notepad, ready to get down to business. "So, tell me a little bit about your grandmother." "My grandmother's name is Hattie, but everyone calls her Hattie Mae. She's seventy-one years old and just recently suffered a stroke. Since then, she has been very forgetful, and has had a few accidents where she left the stove or the oven on. I'm worried she is going to get hurt while I'm away," he said.

"My grandmother became my guardian when I was six years old. One day, I came home from school and my mother told me she was going away for a few days on a trip for work and she never came back.

Occasionally, I would receive a phone call here and there from my mother to check in on us. But, then that eventually stopped."

There was something about the emotion in Lamont's eyes that conveyed the hurt and trauma he had experienced from the neglect of his mother. Giselle couldn't help but speculate if Lamont's womanizing behavior was due to the neglect from his mother. He specified his grandmother's interests, medications, allergies, and favorite foods, making it easy for Giselle to create a proper care plan for her.

"Tamra always talks about how good you are at what you do. I figured I'd hit you up to see if you could help me with Hattie Mae," said Lamont. "She is a sweet old lady, but she can be mean as a snake. I know she isn't going to like the idea of a stranger in her home," he continued. "How soon could you set up a home assessment, so I can tour her home and meet her?" Giselle asked.

Even though she was ready to get the ball rolling, she knew she was overextending herself taking on Hattie Mae's case. However, she was in no position to decline. Her bills and tuition cost were overwhelming her, and she needed all the extra money she could get. "How's today looking for you?" "Today could work. I could meet you there around three," she said, glancing at her phone's calendar, taking notice of all the assignments she had on her to-do list.

"Cool, I'll meet you there at three. Then I'll sign the papers and pay you your fee," Lamont agreed before rushing from the table promptly. He informed Giselle that he had an important business meeting to get to. Which in his language and line of work meant he had a play to run. Under normal circumstances, Giselle would have avoided doing business with a drug dealer, but she needed the money.

She told herself that it wasn't her business how Lamont earned his money, although deep down her moral compass did not agree with that thought process.

Giselle sat at the table, looking over the menu, contemplating what to order. She had been so consumed with work and study that she no longer had a consistent healthy eating regimen. She frequently skipped meals without recognizing it. Her unhealthy lifestyle made food consumption and adequate rest, on her self-care checklist, often unaccounted for. She could feel the burnout flowing through her mind and veins as she sat at the table, forming a merger with restlessness and hunger.

Giselle ordered a salmon salad and a watermelon martini in hopes that the meal and the drink would be enough to satisfy her malnourished state. She pulled out her laptop to input the answers to the questionnaire she had asked Lamont regarding his grandmother. She began typing away, getting lost in her role as the boss when she felt an unusual feeling sweep over her. She glanced around taking notice of the abnormal energy flowing through the air. She didn't know what to make of it, but it was an unusual feeling she had never felt before.

A vision popped into her head as if she were caught in an unusual daydream. Giselle looked around the room and realized she was no longer sitting in the cafe, waiting on her salmon salad. She took notice of the people huddled around in a circle, wearing red hooded robes with their faces hidden from all visibility. She began walking around the room assessing the imagery. One of the hooded seven that stood in the center of the room walked forward.

Signaling a turn of events to the rest of the hooded followers. A child began walking closer and approached the hooded leader, wearing the same red-hooded garment as the others. "Come child," the voice replied from under the hooded robe. "Come closer." The hooded leader waited in silence after the child approached the threshold and watched as the floorboards began to move. Within minutes, a large cubed structure began to emerge from the center of the floor. It appeared to be a cage containing what looked to be a baby goat.

The hooded leader approached the cage, removed the goat, and lead it to the threshold on a leash. The child began to shake with fear as the hooded leader approached her closer and closer. The hooded leader handed the small girl a dagger while restraining the goat in a fixed position. The girl walked closer approaching the constricted goat while her hands and body continued to tremble. She raised the dagger with her right hand that was shaking, prepared to approach the goat when Giselle snapped out of her trance and was back in real-time sitting at the restaurant table.

Giselle looked around the room in a panic. She felt overwhelmed as she panted loudly, as if she had just run a mile in a minute. She looked around the room to observe if there was anything or anyone out of place. She didn't know what to make of her new gift, but she was certain her abilities had a mind of their own. The lack of control was driving Giselle mad. She had been experiencing fatigue, exhaustion, and uncertainty about her future. It was becoming quite inconvenient for her to be dashing in and out of psychic visions so abruptly during important times of the day.

She thought about all of the responsibilities she had on her plate. Was she making a mistake by taking on Hattie Mae's case? What if she went into a vision while working with Hattie? What would happen? There were so many questions and concerns racing in the back of Giselle's mind that she didn't know where to start and where to stop. What she did know was that Christophe was starting to summon her more often than usual.

The first order of business was preparing herself for the offering, because that could be the answer to her financial problems. She was still unclear about a lot that involved the Illuminus Society. But, it was starting to look like being inducted was a part of her destiny and purpose whether she felt mentally and emotionally up for it or not.

Elizabeth's alarm clock chimed. It was time to get up despite her unemployed status. She rolled over prepared to lay soaking in the misery of uncertainty when she smelled the aroma of breakfast floating from the kitchen. She entered the kitchen, wiping the crust from the corner of her eyes as she took notice of the man, dancing in his pajamas and singing while making pancakes. "Your pretty chipper this morning for a man who just got dumped and put out," Elizabeth said to Jonathan after taking notice of how extremely happy he appeared to be despite his situation.

"Misery loves company and the unemployed are never chipper," he said, making a joke sparking a smile from Elizabeth despite her worries about her future. "Now, why don't you bring your jobless energy in here and join me with my homeless energy so we can form a merger and enjoy breakfast and be miserable together," Jonathan continued. "Well, if I would've known you being single and home-less meant breakfast for me and happiness for you, I would have encouraged it a long time ago!" Elizabeth said as she took a bite of the pancake. Jonathan was a great cook and an expert pancake maker. He always managed to make his pancakes the perfect size and texture. Never earning complaints from anyone who consumed them.

"So, what's new?" Asked Elizabeth as she cherished every bite of the delicious breakfast. She had not had breakfast prepared for her since the passing of her mother. So Jonathan preparing her a meal felt very special to her. "Well, I am going to go to the office and attempt to give people relationship advice despite the dynamics of my failed relationship. After that, I plan on coming back here and taking a nap on my best friend's couch. That's how my day is going to look today."

"What about Alicia?" Elizabeth asked with a mouth full of half-chewed pancakes. "What about her?" Jonathan replied as if he had no interest in hearing her name in the context of any conversation. "I just assumed that you would have reached out to her just to see if she's doing ok. I mean despite the events that have transpired you two have been together for a long time. I'm sure it's hard for her to process all of this," Elizabeth suggested. "Just like it's hard for me to process the fact that I am currently being forced to sleep on my best friend's uncomfortable sofa, no offense," Jonathan replied. "None taken," she responded being fully aware of how uncomfortable her sofa truly was.

It was not like Jonathan to be so careless about other people's feelings. Alicia had put him out, but what did he expect her to do? Elizabeth wondered if Jonathan's frustration and anger towards his ex-fiancee was a product of guilt. She took into account that he had stayed in a relationship he was unhappy with for so long that he wanted to place the blame in areas it didn't belong.

The room got silent as they both shoved the food around on their plates and pretended to be consumed with eating. Elizabeth received a notification from her bank mobile app about her account. Dropping her fork onto her plate, she abruptly spit out the portion of food that was still in her mouth. "What's wrong?" Jonathan asked, feeling alarmed after observing the shocked look on Elizabeth's face. "There must be some mistake," she said, ignoring Jonathan's question. He was more concerned when she received another notification on her smartphone.

An image popped up with the Illuminus Crest along with a message telling her, "Congratulations! You have just received your first gift from the Crest of Abundance. We look forward to seeing you at the induction ceremony to properly welcome you into our organization. Together we will continue to push boundaries in a non-inclusive world to continue to build Black Excellence."

"What's wrong?" Jonathan asked again, eager to learn what had transpired that had shaken Elizabeth's demeanor. "You won't believe this," she said as she sat back down in her chair slowly taking it all in. The Illuminus Society just gifted me two hundred thousand dollars. "What?" Jonathan replied, feeling confused. "Why would they do that?" He asked. "I don't know," Elizabeth replied. "I received a notification from my bank that there had been two hundred thousand placed in my account and right after this popped up on my screen," she said. She showed Jonathan the message from the society.

Jonathan wanted badly to let Elizabeth know about the bad feeling he had about the secret society that had just popped into her life out of nowhere. He kept questioning if the society had something to do with Omari's death and if they were more ominous than they appeared to be. Jonathan continued to put pieces together in his head after going over Omari's last session. Omari had been divulging bits and pieces of information about Illuminus. This information gave Jonathan the impression that the society didn't turn out to be as good as Omari had hoped.

It made sense to Jonathan why Elizabeth would be a good candidate for a cult-like society that operated under the guise of building Black Excellence. She was a single woman with no real support system who was now newly unemployed. What didn't make sense to him is why an organization would give someone a lump sum of cash who hadn't been inducted in. Jonathan kept his concerns to himself while he sat and pretended to be happy for his friend.

"Well would you look at that. Once again God has provided," he said while planting a false smile on his face. "Now you can take your time and figure out what it is you truly want to do with your life before you hop back into the job market, looking for your next career endeavor," said Jonathan.

He had told Elizabeth he planned to go into the office to help clients for the day, but suddenly he was feeling a different desire come to mind. Karen Black had shared her opinions of Omari's death with Jonathan. This made it even clearer to him that there was more to the story than the so-called robbery the news had been reporting. Jonathan couldn't shake the notion that the Illuminus Society had something to do with Omari's murder. He wanted to be happy for Elizabeth's new blessing, but something was telling him the blessings and offer were all too good to be true.

What was their real agenda? What did they want with Elizabeth? Jonathan didn't know what was going on. However, he was determined now more than ever to find out. He said goodbye to Elizabeth, and rushed out of the door to get to work. He left Elizabeth sitting at the breakfast table consumed with looking at her account balance.

She was unaware that she was the first to receive the offering and would soon be required to do something immoral in return for the financial gift. She heard a loud thump onto the front porch. It sent her outside immediately where she was greeted by a package delivery man dressed in uniform with an Illuminus crest pierced in the top right breast area of his uniform. "Have a good evening and enjoy," he said as he hopped back into the vehicle and drove away quickly.

Elizabeth picked up the package covered in red wrapping paper and a black bow. She unwrapped the contents fairly slowly. Inside the package was a name tag suitable for a work desk with her name engraved in gold letters. Attached was a smaller envelope with a note on the inside. Elizabeth opened the note to find that she was offered a job as the lead financial advisor and account specialist at the Illuminus Society.

Elizabeth couldn't believe her eyes. Two phenomenal blessings in one day, she thought to herself as she began to cry silently thankful to God for providing an answer to her problems. Elizabeth would soon learn that not all things that appear to be blessings are, and not all blessings are from God. For the devil was a provider as well.

10

Not Your Average Karen

Jonathan arrived in the parking lot of his office. He continued to feel plagued with thoughts of the Illuminus Society, and what role they could have potentially played in Omari's Murder. Decapitating a person was a heinous act of violence. He didn't believe a robber would have the time or desire to behead a man after swiping his valuables. "Good Morning, Taylor," he said as he walked into his office.

He was startled by the dark-skinned woman who sat silently on the sofa, awaiting his arrival. "I'm sorry, Ms. Black, but you frightened me. Taylor didn't mention to me that I had anyone waiting for me." "That's because she didn't know," Black replied casually as she waited for Jonathan to get settled. "You ran out of here last week pretty fast, and I have been meaning to check back in with you to see if you were doing ok." "I'm doing fine, but I am not here for myself," she said, making it clear to Jonathan that the discussion of their last session was far away from being the focus of her unannounced visit.

"I am here because I wanted to talk to you about Omari Bronson. I've been doing some digging. It turns out Omari may have gotten himself into some trouble after joining a cult." Jonathan looked up at Black in shock of her allegations. What could she possibly know about Illuminus, he wondered as he continued to listen to her divulge information.

After hearing an overload of suspicious hearsay from Black, he asked, "Have you told the police what you know?" "No, I have not. The Illuminus Society is highly connected, and one visit to the police could put me in harm's way. It will also alert Omari's killer that I'm on to them. I came to you, because I was able to get a hold of his cell phone records and emails. Three days before he was killed, he received emails from a member of the Illuminus Society, warning him that they were aware of his sessions with you. Apparently, some-one had informed them that he had been divulging details about the society to you. I think that may have gotten him killed."

Jonathan looked puzzled he had never breached any of his clients' confidentiality agreements, and never discussed clients with his ex-fiancé. He did not understand who could have possi-bly been aware of the details that Omari had been sharing with him prior to his murder. "The only person who has ever been present when Omari came for his sessions were me and my receptionist, Taylor," he said out loud to make sense of the new information he received.

"Is there any possibility she could be linked to Illuminus?" Black asked. "Taylor? Hell nah," Jonathan said in a casual tone not wanting to link the pretty young receptionist to the sinister society without heavy motive or evidence. "Is that a definite hell no or an I don't know?" She asked as she attempted to make sense of the information. "That's a definite hell no! Taylor has been working for me since I started my practice. She is reliable and honest. I can't believe she would jeopardize me or my clients in any way."

Black could hear the defensiveness in Jonathan's voice so she decided to keep going. "Have you ever noticed her or any of your clients wearing one of these?" She asked. She held up the same crest-shaped pin he had found in his office. "No, I have not. But, I did find one of those a few days ago when I was cleaning out my office." "Is it possible that Taylor could have been in your office snooping around and dropped the crest?" Black asked.

Jonathan paused putting pieces together he did not want to admit were well fit. "There's a possibility. But what would she possibly hope to find in my office?" he asked rhetorically. "Omari's file, which I would assume has all of the information about you two's sessions," said Black.

Jonathan stood up from his chair ready to go and questioned Taylor to see what she knew when Black stopped him in his tracks. "Wait, if Taylor is the culprit, and she is working for the Illuminus Society, she can be valuable to us." "What do you mean?" Jonathan asked confused as to what she was getting at. "Think about it. Omari was tied in with the society. I would imagine you have plenty of other high-end clients who are linked to the society. Omari was breaking. That's why he came to talk to you. I would assume that there will be others. If all else fails, I have been offered an invitation so we can use that to bait Taylor in to catch her when she's doing the next sweep through your files. Then boom, nail her, apply pressure, and find out everything she knows about Illuminus," Black concluded.

"But what if she doesn't break?" he asked. "Trust me. She will. I am going to make sure of it." Black said with confidence. "My friend was offered an invitation, too. This morning she received two hundred thousand dollars from them without any prior commitment being made." "That's the offering. The society will offer each of its inductees a significant financial offering, but it comes with a price. The inductee will be required to do something to prove their loyalty to Illuminus, by taking on an act of immorality that is selected by the leader.

Black had confirmed all of Jonathan's suspicions about the society. This information led him to believe that Elizabeth might have been in danger. He had never known Elizabeth to hold a secret. Judging from the way she had been divulging information to him about her invite and offering, it was clear she had no idea what she was getting herself into.

"What do you think we can do?" He asked. "I'm not sure yet. But, I've been doing some digging and it appears there may be several other murders attached to the society. Black pulled out a folder, spreading pictures of six corpses that had been mutilated, decapitated, and disfigured in many different ways. This was nineteen-year-old rap star, Gabrielle Tunes. She was signed to a record label that was linked to Illuminus and believed to have been a hired snooper for the society as well. Gabrielle was signed a year ago and came up quickly after being inducted into the society. Gabrielle's body was found mutilated inside of an abandoned building along with drugs and money and was staged to look like a drug deal gone wrong."

"Gabrielle's sister told police in a statement, back in October, that Gabrielle had divulged to her that she had become tied in with a secret society known as Illuminus. She was afraid after failing to complete a task that was required of her that she would soon end up dead. The sister said Gabrielle had given her this pin a week before being murdered and told her to show this to the police if anything were to happen to her. The police took her statement and the crest, and a few months later the case went cold."

"Photo two is of a Howard University graduate and a prominent business lawyer named Maxwell Davenport. Thirty-three-year-old Davenport is believed to have been a member of the Illuminus Society for the past nine years. It is unclear what went wrong in Davenport's situation with Illuminus. He was found six months ago murdered at his desk. All of his fingers, toes, and tongue had been severed, all mailed to his home address three weeks later. The package was found and opened by his then pregnant wife."

"According to the investigator, who took the wife's statement, the wife seemed shaken up and anxious. It's noted here in the case file that Mrs. Davenport seemed jumpy and suspicious like she was hiding something. I went to speak with the investigator who happens to be a friend of mine, and she told me she couldn't shake the feeling that Mrs. Davenport knew more than what she had shared with the police. She also believed that she may have known who killed her husband and was being threatened."

Jonathan stood frozen with shock as he watched Black continue to go through the rest of the photos, sharing what information she had about each candidate and the details of their murder. He was now more worried than ever. He had to share what he knew about Illuminus with Elizabeth so he could keep her from making one of the biggest mistakes of her life. "I have to warn Elizabeth," he said aloud. He felt overwhelmed by all of the information. "No! You can't do that," She said firmly. "She has to go through with the induction process whether you want her to or not. She's already received the offering, if she declines they will kill her."

"The Illuminus Society has been a well-oiled machine for many generations. It has helped African-Americans achieve greatness while remaining a secret to the rest of the world. I believe many if not all of these people got themselves killed because they put that secret at risk, and Illuminus is covering their tracks making it appear as if they were robbed, involved in drug dealings or worse. I spoke with Gabrielle's family and friends, all of whom confirmed that she never drank, did drugs, or sold drugs in her life. Apparently, the community she comes from is a very tight-knit community where everyone knows everyone and everyone knows everyone's business. I know you may not want to hear this, but if we are going to find out what happened to Omari and the others, and bring Illuminus down, your friend Elizabeth could be of great use to us. Having two sets of eyes on the inside is better than one. I will be there looking out for her," Black assured.

Jonathan took a deep breath as he processed what it was Black was conjuring up. Elizabeth was fragile. He did not want to do something to harm the authenticity of their friendship or put her in harm's way. Nevertheless, he knew he didn't have many options outside of Black's plan.

"The induction is in three days. After that, our plan is in motion. We will wait it out. Until then, after I get in, and I feel like they trust me, you can inform Elizabeth of what's going on. Between the two of us, we should be able to get some answers. Then we bait Taylor in, and set up hidden cameras in and outside of your office. The next time she does her snooping, I'll pounce! Then, I'll drain her of everything she knows and find out what the Illuminus society really is and what they want with us. And, why they killed Omari!" Black concluded. She spoke with a level of bravery and confidence Jonathan had never heard present in a woman before. It was clear. Her time working as a special agent had made her more than well equipped to get to the bottom of things.

He couldn't believe that someone so young and helpful as Taylor could have been playing him the entire time. If Taylor was a member of Illuminus what was she hoping to gain and why did they choose his establishment as a place of interest? He started replaying all of the information Black had unloaded on him. He realized he had not asked her the most important question of all. "How do you know all of this?" Jonathan asked. "You say the Illuminus Society is very secretive and intricate. Yet, you seem to know a whole lot about them. I'm wondering how." "Let's just say I'm not your average Karen. We will talk soon," she said, smiling at Jonathan as she exited his office, leaving him with even more questions than he originally had before her visit. Agent Karen Black was interesting and mysterious to him, and she was right. She was definitely not the average Karen!

11

More Money, More Problems

Alicia laid in bed feeling insignificant. She felt the sting of depression after taking into account that she would not be walking down the aisle with Jonathan as she had planned. Ever since his departure, she had remained glued to her bed, crying and replaying all of the events in her life. She wondered what she could have done to change his mind.

Alicia refused fluid and food each time her mother offered. The doorbell rang, but Alicia did not move. Betty rushed to the door praying it would be someone paying Alicia a visit that could influence her to get out of bed. She opened the door happily, relieved to see Tamra standing in the doorway with flowers and a bottle of wine. "Thank the Lord!" Betty yelled out as she invited Tamra in.

"Is it that bad?" Tamra asked as she entered the large home, sitting her designer bag on the table. She looked around and noticed all of the new decor that had been added since her last visit. "What's up with her? I've been calling her phone for days and she has not answered one call," Tamra stated in a frustrated tone. "She's been laying in the bed ever since Jonathan left. Crying nonstop. I can't get her to eat one bite of food," Betty said as she started tearing up.

"I don't know what to do. I tried to warn her that he wasn't right for her. He's taken everything he could take from her to get on his feet. And, now he's dropped her on her head like he has not got one care in the world for her or her feelings. Her father and I always tried to teach her the importance of surrounding herself with people of the same class as her. "Well, damn. How did I squeeze my way in here then?" Tamra asked jokingly.

Tamra and Betty had always had a close relationship. Tamra felt as though they were just as much of friends as she and Alicia were. "You know I don't mean it in that way," Betty said, laughing along with Tamra. "Of course, I do, Mrs. Betty. I was simply trying to lighten your load with a laugh. We all knew Jonathan and Alicia weren't going to work out. A blind man could see that. She was always more invested in him than he was in her."

"There were numerous situations where your daughter and I had planned things together. We'd see the plans through, and have the best time. When Jonathan came into her life, all of that changed. She stopped coming to my house to get her hair done regularly, because Jonathan told her he didn't want her wearing extensions. Next thing I knew, she started going to Rocky's shop once in a blue moon, getting haircuts and questioning her about locs." "Alicia would never loc her hair," Betty replied.

Tamara continued, "I kept my opinions to myself. Because, your daughter doesn't like to be told anything. Especially, when it comes to that man! The year Jonathan was due to graduate from school, I had run into some financial problems. I went to Alicia hoping she could help me out. I asked her to borrow ten thousand dollars to help me get out of a bind so I could still have enough money to open my shop. Alicia told me she would help. A week passed and she messaged me one day saying she could no longer let me borrow the money she had promised. A month later Jonathan opened his practice with her money, I'm sure."

"What! Why didn't you ever mention this to me? Robert and I would have helped you out." Betty interjected. "I couldn't do that. I know how Alicia is, and I didn't want any problems with my friend. So, I skipped out on the idea of opening my own shop, and I watched her pour all of her time and money into helping a man she knew was only in it for the resources she provided him with. I talked to her several times about us making business moves together. But, sure enough, Jonathan would always block. He was scared I was going to get a resource from Alicia that he wanted which was usually in the form of a dollar bill or time."

Betty sat listening to Tamra vent, shaking her head. "All of that to help a man who never even wanted to be her man," Betty concluded. "Exactly my point," Tamra said. "Now he's run off with her money, her time, and everything she has ever invested in him. You know who's here to clean up his mess and actually show some love and care for her….me!"

Betty hated hearing about the kind of things Alicia had done to Tamra all to please a man who had no real intentions of growing with her. "Robert and I told her it was not going to work. She would always try to argue us down, saying we didn't like him because he didn't have anything. When the truth was, we didn't want them together, because we could see he was a user. We could see they weren't equally yoked. He had become entirely too comfortable with Alicia taking care of him, funding his dreams and endeavors while he didn't reciprocate five percent of what she put out," said Betty.

Before she could speak another word Alicia came roaming in slowly looking like the walking dead. She startled both of them. Her hair was matted and tangled, she was dressed in a pair of frumpy charcoal-colored sweats and a wrinkled graphic t-shirt. "I know you guys are in here talking about me," she said, in a distorted voice. "You know what you have every right to be mad at me for the things I did. I put Jonathan before everyone and everything. Now, he's off shacking up with Elizabeth while I'm left in this big house with nothing but my designer wardrobe and my judgmental mother," she said, appearing to have some displaced animosity towards Betty who had been there taking care of her on a daily basis.

"Now, slow down Licia. I know you're hurting., but you can't take your frustrations out on Betty. All your mother has done from the beginning is try to look out for you," Tamra interjected. Before Alicia could open her mouth to respond she fell to the floor and collapsed abruptly. Her body laid still. Betty screamed to the top of her lungs. She rushed to Alicia's aide. "Call the ambulance!" She's not breathing! Why is she not breathing?" Betty yelled, holding Alicia in her lap while Tamra called 911.

Tamra began pacing and looking around the house while she gave the operator all the information she could describing Alicia's collapse. The 911 operator asked her a series of questions about Alicia. This lead her to enter Alicia's room where she found a bottle of oxycodone that was completely empty with the lid resting beside the bottle on her nightstand. The bottle appeared to belong to Alicia's father, Robert. Tamra carried the empty bottle out to the sitting room where Betty and Tamra were still planted on the floor. She showed Betty the empty bottle. "I think she may have taken these," Tamra said as she heard the front door open and the paramedics entered rushing to Alicia's aide.

The paramedics performed CPR and Alicia came to. They placed Alicia's body onto the stretcher and headed out the door. Tamra informed them that she had potentially taken an overdose. She gave them the pill bottle. Betty rushed over to Tamra frigidly filled with anxiety. "I'm going to go with her," she said as if Tamra had assumed otherwise. "Could you stay here and get the house in order for her, so she can be comfortable when she gets discharged." "Of course," Tamra said. Betty handed Tamra a spare key, instructing her to lock up and hold onto the key when she was finished.

Tamra started in Alicia's bedroom. She stripped the sheets and removed the trash from the room. Her phone rang. "Hello," she said, happy to hear Giselle's voice on the other end. "What are you up to?" asked Giselle. "I don't think I even wanna say," said Tamra. "I hadn't heard from Alicia for a while because she wasn't picking up any of my calls. So, I decided to pop up on her. Her mother and I were talking for a while in the living room. Betty was filling me in on how depressed Alicia had been since Jonathan left. Before we knew it, she walked into the room, talking out of her head, and collapsed to the floor. I went into her room and found an empty bottle of Oxy's by her bed. I'm guessing she took them all and that's why she passed out." "What! Are you serious?" Giselle asked, feeling concerned for Alicia. "I know love is blind, but it can't be that blind that you try to kill yourself," Giselle added.

"Is she gonna be okay?" asked Giselle. "I don't know. I'm gonna stay at her place and try to get it in order for her. Maybe pick her up some groceries. Are you busy right now? If not, you think you could swing over and help me out? Maybe pick up a few groceries, and I pay you back when you get here," Tamra added. "I'm still at Hattie Mae's. Lamont texted me over an hour ago and said he was on his way. He still hasn't gotten here. That's why I was calling you," Giselle replied. "Ughh, he is so damn tacky. I will give him a call for you," replied Tamra. "Thanks, girl. I hate to involve you. But, I didn't know who else to call. I'll head over there to help you out as soon as Lamont gets here."

Giselle hated informing Tamra about Lamont being late but it was now going on the fourth occasion he had done so. He had ignored all of her calls and text which broke the contract agreement he had signed.

Lamont came rushing through the door. As he apologized, his phone started to ring repeatedly followed by text message notifications. He glanced at the phone and took notice of all of the insulting text messages he had received from Tamra within minutes; chewing him out, and accusing him of taking advantage of her cousin, Giselle. "So, that's how it is?" he asked, looking at Giselle with a surprised look plastered on his face. "What do you mean?" She asked. "So you're reporting to Tamra about me now?" He asked. "That's exactly how it is Lamont," she replied with an attitude present in her voice that he had never heard before.

"This is the fourth time you've been late. I hate to break it to you, but the world doesn't revolve around you. I have other clients I need to be checking in with, employees to speak to, and schoolwork that needs to be done. So, I hate to inform you that I, Giselle Howard, am not and can not be on your time!" There was something about the straightforward sense of assertiveness in Giselle's tone that made Lamont feel a way he had never felt before. He approached Giselle slowly, repetitively expressing how sorry he was letting her know it was not his intention to take advantage of her.

"Chile don't listen to him, all he knows how to do is be late. Probably gonna show up to my funeral late with his pants falling off his behind," added Hattie Mae. Giselle laughed as she tried to hold her angry facial expression in place when making eye contact with Lamont to convey to him that the way he had done things previously was not ok. "I apologize and promise I will be on time from here on out. Why don't I walk you outside while you wait for your Uber," said Lamont. His goal was to lessen Giselle's anger toward him.

She said goodbye to Hattie Mae as Lamont walked her outside to wait for her Uber. Hattie Mae awaited their exit, making her way over to the window, glancing out to get a glimpse of the two young people.

Giselle stood in complete silence, pretending to look at her phone when Lamont tried to spark a conversation.

"You know I really admire your ambition," he said, making his way closer to her. "You were pretty upset with me today, and I wanna apologize again. It was never my intention to disrespect you, or make you feel like I was taking advantage." "You said that already," she replied, appearing to be uninterested in the conversation. "Well, I wanted to say it again," he said as he moved closer.

"You know originally I told you that I hired you because I knew you were good at what you do, but that was a lie." "Excuse me?" Giselle said, feeling offended by Lamont's statement. "No. Well, I mean it wasn't a lie. You are good at what you do, but that's not why I hired you." "Well if that wasn't the reason you hired me, then what was?" Giselle questioned in an offended tone.

"I hired you because I think you're a beautiful person, and I wanted to get to know you. Don't get me wrong. You're good at what you do, but I wasn't interested in that. I've been around a lot of women, but never anyone like you. You're quiet, composed, classy, and smart. It also doesn't hurt that you're fine as hell, and I always wanted to get a closer look at you. I hired you to see if what I was observing was real."

Giselle was floored by the words that were coming out of Lamont's mouth. "How can you say all of this when you know me and Tamra are cousins?" She inquired. "Tamra is cool, don't get me wrong. But, she already knows what it is with me and her. I know that's your cousin. I wouldn't ever want to come between y'all. But, Giselle I can't hide how I feel about you. Every time you came around, I would get this funny feeling, and I couldn't keep my eyes off you. I understand if you're not interested. I am just trying to keep it real with you," he said as he grabbed her hand kissing it gently.

Leaning in closer, and closer until he was close enough for his lips to meet hers. He stole a kiss that Giselle knew was wrong, but she could not manage to break away from. As he leaned in more he kissed her again. Her body language spoke to him in a way her words could not. Giselle and Lamont stood kissing enthralled in complete bliss when the Uber driver approached beeping the horn aggressively, ruining the moment and bringing them back to reality.

"Shit!" Giselle said after she recognized the Uber driver. She hopped into the Uber without saying anything more to Lamont. "Hello," the Uber driver said, greeting Giselle with a smile. "I see you're off to the grocery store. You preparing dinner for one tonight or two?" The Uber driver asked sarcastically as she popped her gum in between sentences. Giselle did not respond, ignoring the driver's attempt to get under her skin. "I don't wanna pry, but why did you tell me that was your cousin's man when he is obviously yours?" Mia asked. "If I offended you, I didn't mean to," she said waiting for Giselle to respond, but she said nothing.

Giselle sat in the back of the Uber feeling horrible. It was not like her to be scandalous. She loved Tamra with all of her heart. How could she allow Lamont to swindle her into letting him kiss her? She wondered. Had she been sleep-deprived for so long that she could no longer make a sound decision? It also wasn't making her situation any better that the Uber driver who happened to have a previous situation with Lamont had spotted them in the act. Giselle didn't know who

Mia would mention it to, but she knew she needed to tell Tamra before someone else did.

"We're here," Mia said, pulling up to the grocery store, sounding even more chipper than before. "Would you like for me to wait on you?" she asked, holding a condescending phony smile. She could tell from Giselle's demeanor she was not interested in riding with her anywhere else. "No, thank you," Giselle responded as she approved the final payment tipping her pessimistic driver one dollar out of spite. "Witch!" Mia replied under her breath as the door to the vehicle closed. She drove away, feeling accomplished after her petty exchange.

As Giselle approached the fruit aisle deep in thought about her immoral exchange with Lamont, she received a text notification, informing her that four hundred thousand dollars had been deposited into her account. The notification was followed by a message alert of confetti, exploding across her smartphone screen with the Illuminus crest in the background. "You have received your financial offering from us here at Illuminus. We look forward to seeing you at the induction," the message read.

Giselle's head started spinning, as she tried to figure out why an organization would give her such a large amount of money. Then she remembered what Christophe had told her. She stood still, preparing to be summoned by the old man, but nothing happened. She looked around the store and noticed a young man who appeared to be watching her.

Giselle continued to walk down the aisle. She entered the bread aisle and acted as if she was not watching the young hooded man who appeared to still have his eyesight set on her. He followed her into each aisle as she made her way through the store picking up the groceries Tamra had requested.

Giselle looked over her shoulder. She made her way to the checkout line. She looked around. The young man was nowhere in sight. She thought she had officially gone off the deep end and lost what little marbles she had left. She grabbed her grocery cart and headed for the door to wait for her Uber. She went over all of the chaotic events of the day; from kissing Lamont to the large lump sum of cash deposited into her account. She realized the kiss could have been the immoral act Christophe had warned her about. Giselle obsessed over wrapping her mind around all that had occurred when her Uber arrived. She prepared to put her groceries in the trunk when a young man hopped out offering to do it for her. Giselle thanked him, hopping into the back of the Uber while he loaded the trunk for her.

Just yesterday, she had been worried about her finances and it appeared the Illuminus Society had now stripped her of those worries. Kissing Lamont had crossed lines she didn't believe in crossing, and she knew she could no longer work for him. She decided, at that moment, she would strip Lamont of his abilities to try to run any more games on her by quitting. She had grown fond of Hattie Mae, but it was what she knew had to be done.

"Are you doing okay?" The driver asked. "You look like you have a lot on your mind." "Today has been a longggg day," Giselle replied. "I know how that is. I was having a day like that last week," the young man responded. Giselle couldn't help but notice how familiar the voice sounded coming from behind the steering wheel. "Do I know you from somewhere?" Giselle asked. "Not to my knowledge. But, hello nice to meet you…" He replied. "Giselle…Giselle Howard," she said. "I'm Kyle," he responded. "Nice to meet you, Kyle, and thanks for helping me with my groceries," Giselle said. She was relieved that the Uber driver was someone other than Mia.

Giselle kept replaying the day over and over in her mind while she rode consumed with silence in the back of the Uber while Kyle continued to steal glances at her in his rearview mirror. There were so many things she wished she could have done over when Lamont approached her outside of his home. Why did he feel the need to kiss her out of all of the girls Tamra had brought around?

She thought about how he had told her he felt a vibe from her that was different from all the other girls. What is so different about me? She questioned. I just let him kiss me knowing he is in a relationship with Tamra. Obviously, I'm not so different she thought in disgust. Tamra had been there for her since day one and it was a hard pill to swallow to know that she had done such a treacherous thing.

Kyle glanced at Giselle in the mirror. He felt the urge to pull the car over and tell her who he was, and await her response. He was getting tired of following and watching her from a distance. There she sat in the backseat of his car plagued with thoughts that he wanted so badly to know more about. He wondered if she had an idea about what was happening to her, and if she had now figured out how her powers worked. With every stolen glance, Kyle wondered how a mother could give up such a beautiful human. Giselle had brown skin, big wide glossy eyes, full lips, and her facial features were noticeably attractive. He wondered if she had inherited her intelligence from their mother or if that was simply a thing he did not have the pleasure of knowing for himself.

Kyle pulled into Alicia's driveway slowly. He dreaded his departure from the sister he wanted to know more about. Giselle thanked him, as she exited the Uber before he stopped her. "I don't know if or when you'll be needing a ride again, but here's my card," he said, smiling as she took the business card from his hand.

Giselle grabbed the grocery bags and rang the doorbell repeatedly before Tamra approached the door. "Girl, what took you so long?" Tamra asked as she helped Giselle carry in the groceries. "I'm almost finished cleaning the entire downstairs area. And, let me just say that Alicia is a lot messier than she lets on. They clearly need to hire a better housekeeper," Tamra said as she blabbed on and on not taking notice of Giselle's lack of attention to what she was saying.

Giselle felt like such a fraud sitting there with Tamra after what she had done. She wanted to come out and tell her, but she knew Tamra would never forgive her. So, she sat in silence zoned out while Tamra continued. "Selle! Selle," she yelled again, breaking Giselle's concentration. "Is everything okay?" Asked Tamra, finally taking notice that Giselle was a million miles away.

"I'm okay. Today has just been a long day." Giselle couldn't make sense of any of it. The kiss, the offering, and her betrayal against her favorite person. What was she becoming? Had she finally cracked from burnout, and now she was just another person willing to do anything to get what she needed? She sat and stared at her mobile banking app counting the zeros. She couldn't fathom how all of the things Christophe had warned her about were currently coming into play. She looked at the offering and questioned why someone would give her such a large amount of money.

Tamra glanced over at Giselle's phone to see what was holding her attention. When her eyes began to bulge out of her head. "How did you get all of that money?" Tamra asked. She was shocked her little cousin had built more financial stability than what she had originally assumed. Giselle looked up at her cousin and took notice of the odd expression planted on her face.

Tamra looked as if she was mad, but Giselle did not understand why. Growing up Giselle never had as much as Tamra because her mother was a single mom. Tamra would walk around in the best of the best after her parents hit the lottery. Her parents moved their family into a large suburban home, and gave Tamra a life they had never known before the score the lottery ticket had blessed them with. Tamra's parents spoiled her rotten. They helped her to evolve into a person that was selfish, self-centered, and self-absorbed.

A few years after the win, Tamra's parents lost everything. This forced Tamra to conform to a less lavish lifestyle than what she was used to. This caused her numerous issues and an elevated sense of jealousy anytime it appeared that the people around her were having financial gains that she was not. Tamra and Rocky were no longer friends due to that fact. Tamra had become jealous after seeing Rocky open a salon before she could, and it made her furious. She constantly took shots at Rocky's hairstylist capabilities anytime Giselle came around after getting a new do at Rocky's salon.

"Girl, this whole time you have been walking around complaining and worried about money, and you have that kind of money in your bank account," Tamra said with a level of animosity present in her voice. Tamra had always been there for Giselle as a listener, but nothing more. Giselle knew she couldn't disclose the details of how she got the money without blowing her cover and violating the number one rule of the Illuminus Society. She stayed quiet while Tamra continued on. "You know I've been trying to open a salon, struggling with my bills and you are walking around with hundreds of thousands of dollars in the bank, and you never offered to help me out."

There it was, Giselle thought silently. How could Tamra rant and rave about not receiving a form of help she was never willing to give. It was just like her to act as if she was owed something from any and everyone when it was convenient. The money had been in Giselle's life for less than three hours, and it was already causing her issues. Tamra rambled over and over, acting as if she had been done wrong in some way. Giselle wanted to sit quietly and just take it, but she knew she could not.

"Tamra, I haven't had the money for that long." "It doesn't matter how long you've had it. Don't you think you should've thought of me and offered? One hundred thousand dollars would change my life," Tamra said as she looked at Giselle with disgust. Giselle couldn't believe what she was hearing. How could Tamra approach her with such a bogus request? She had never done anything to help anyone out. Yet, she always managed to find a way to feel entitled to favors and blessings she was unwilling to give.

"Tamra, I understand you're having money problems, but look

around you, we all do. This money was placed into my account this morning. News flash, my dear entitled cousin, it hasn't been a full twenty-four hours yet. You really think I'm focused on what other people need right now? When I barely can keep track of what I need. I've been on my own for so long working around the clock. I've struggled to keep my business afloat and my bills paid, and you want to talk to me about needs? Where were you when I needed money to avoid getting evicted? Where were you when I needed money to pay my tuition? Or better yet, where were you when grandma died, and we needed money for a proper burial?" Tamra froze in place and felt the sting of Giselle's inquiry as she took into account the point that was being made.

"Grandma died and I had to take everything I had in my savings and pay for her funeral. Alone! While I watched you post selfies of your trips on social media; Tamra Howard in Dubai, then Cali, then Saint Martin. I was stuck working to rebuild my life without any support system or resources. While you squandered through the rest of your family's lottery money, and lived your best life unconcerned about anyone's needs, but your own. I couldn't come to you then, so it's absurd for you to feel like I owe you something now," Giselle concluded as she watched her cousin continue to be at a complete loss for words.

Giselle didn't care about the money or even helping Tamra. It was the way Tamra had conducted herself after seeing the bank summary that made Giselle respond aggressively. Tamra's self-entitled energy had somehow made Giselle forget about the kiss between her and Lamont.

Tamra stood in the middle of the room uncertain of what to say. She recognized Giselle had made several great points. She had never done anything for anyone other than Alicia; always running to Alicia's aide at the drop of a dime while Alicia treated her as if she was disposable. Tamra had never sensed any animosity from Giselle towards her in reference to their grandmother's funeral. But, it made perfectly good sense to her how she could feel the way she did. Tamra had never cared about anyone other than Lamont and Alicia. Neither of them treated her as if she was of any value at all.

It was at that very moment, after being scolded by Giselle for her behavior, that Tamra realized she was the epitome of selfish. How could she be upset about Giselle's earnings when she saw how hard she had been working for years? Giselle had never known the luxury of a day off or a vacation, while Tamra lived the good life until her parents' money ran out.

Tamra thought back on an argument she had with their grandmother, Edith, before she passed. She envisioned Edith telling her she was a selfish brat, who would never get anywhere until she learned how to consider someone other than herself. It had always been easier to think of Lamont, because he was her boyfriend. Or Alicia, because Alicia was rich, connected, and a good resource in any social setting. But, why hadn't she ever thought about Giselle or worried about her in the same facet as she did the other important people in her life? The answer was simple. She didn't worry about Giselle, because she always knew Giselle would figure things out for herself as she had always done before and after their grandmother's death. No one worries about the person who knows how to handle themself. Tamra realized it was Giselle's ability to always hold her own that made her so easy to overlook. How inconsiderate was she to feel entitled to Giselle's finances, when she had never given Giselle a penny. Yet, there she stood in her rich best friend's home, cleaning and helping, yet again.

For had the shoe been on the other foot, Alicia would not have done the same. She was a hypocrite, and she felt every word that Giselle had spoken to her. She needed to apologize but there was something standing in her way. Perhaps it was the fact that her cousin had now come into hundreds of thousands of dollars, and she was still broke, hustling, and saving for a hair salon that she was starting to feel she'd never achieve.

Giselle grabbed her bag and headed for the door. She was prepared to leave without saying another word. She and Tamra had been through many ups and downs over the years, and she had somehow managed to forget how self-entitled her cousin could be. It was predictably the typical Tamra fashion for her to feel like someone owed her something that they did not. In the past, Giselle had fallen victim to Tamra's tantrums. She had made herself a promise after going through their grandmother's death alone that she would never feel as though she owed Tamra anything ever again. Their relationship was important to her, but not so important that she should find herself required to give into ridiculous requests.

She exited Alicia's home not hearing so much as a goodbye or an I'll call you later from her cousin, making it clear to her where they stood upon her departure. Giselle couldn't help but ponder over the fact that she was broke a few hours ago. She now had come into a new financial situation that had already brought her problems with one of the most important people in her life. She hated leaving Tamra in the way she did, but what more could either party say? It was not the norm for Tamra to understand her wrongs or apologize. Giselle knew the longer she stayed there, the more she would want to say.

Giselle glanced at the bank balance once more. More money, more problems, she thought to herself as she hopped into the Uber headed home for some much needed rest and relaxation.

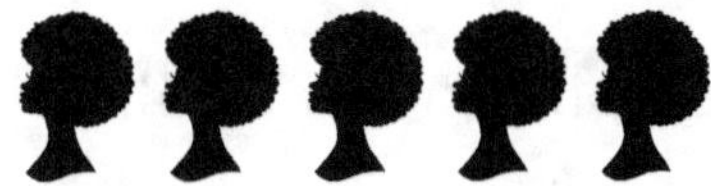

12

The Vulnerable

Magnus entered the main room of the Illuminus mansion prepared to critique the setup for the big day. He managed to recruit a scientist, lawyer, financial representative, actress, and a few other prestigious African-Americans who were all destined for greatness. Magnus made his way towards the first table setting. A loud voice began to pierce through the speakers. "Magnus report to the common room at once. We have to talk," the Queen Mother demanded in an urgent tone.

What could they possibly need to talk about, he wondered as he made his way anxiously to the area she suggested. He was plagued with worries and concerns. Today was the big day, and he could not afford any mistakes or disappointments. He urged the entire house to come together to check and analyze every corner of the Illuminus mansion as they prepared for the new inductees.

Magnus approached the common room surprised to see several other Illuminus members seated and awaiting Queen mothers instructions. "I'm sure you all are wondering what you're doing here," the loud voice said as it continued to pierce through the surround sound speakers. "It has been brought to my attention that there have been questions asked about our former inductee, Omari Bronson. Omari received many blessings while being a member of our society. As a result of that, we did what we do here at Illuminus. We protected the group. After all, we can't have one rotten apple spoiling the lot. So, we did what had to be done. The police are asking questions and I need you all to see to it that they don't find any answers," the Queen Mother instructed. "We will dedicate all of our attention to the

induction ceremony tonight. After that, I will give you all individual instructions on what I need from you." The Queen Mother concluded and dismissed the entire room except for Magnus.

"Magnus, I have a last-minute invitation I would like for you to hand deliver to a young woman who I would like to join the new group of members tonight. She is currently in the hospital after attempting suicide. I need you to think of a way to get her an invitation without being noticed. I will send her information to you. I need you to take care of it right away." Magnus agreed to do as he was told. He found it odd that Queen Mother was interested in adding a last-minute inductee as well as one who was suicidal. What ability could this young lady possibly possess that would allow the Queen Mother to look past her flawed and detrimental mental state? As alarmed as he felt he knew better than to question any of her requests. He headed over to the hospital to find a way to influence the disheveled young lady to join the induction ceremony that was taking place in a few hours.

Giselle hopped out of the shower and slipped on a pair of floral pajamas. She pulled out the cosmetics she needed to prepare herself for the induction, and glanced at her phone. There were two missed calls. She ignored the urge to open the notification in fear it was Tamra. She was in no rush to speak with her after the previous day's event. Giselle experienced a load of mixed emotions due to Tamra's selfish, and entitled behavior. She also felt disappointed in herself for allowing Lamont to kiss her behind Tamra's back. So, for now, distance seemed like the best option.

Giselle felt sluggish and unprepared for the induction ceremony. Her week had been filled with completing numerous tasks and an unusual amount of drama that had deprived her of the mental energy she needed to get through the rest of the week. She was starting to listen to her body in ways she hadn't in the past. She felt like a nap could help her to prepare for the ceremony. Giselle climbed in bed and glanced at her phone again and watched as her notifications piled up significantly. She turned her phone off, dedicating the next few hours to rest to give her mind and body the break it so desperately desired.

Jonathan pulled up to his office prepared to place cameras in every crease and crevice possible in hopes to catch Taylor in the act of snooping through his client files. His phone chimed. It was a message from Betty to inform him that Alicia had attempted an overdose. Jonathan froze in place and felt the sting of shock as he re-read the text hoping to have been mistaken.

He did not want to be with Alicia, but it was never his intention to cause her harm upon his departure. Jonathan was at a loss for words. He had never known Alicia to be helpless or suicidal. He couldn't help but feel at fault for her drastic decision. His mother had always taught him to value and cherish the women in his life. Although he had chosen to leave Alicia, he knew he should be by her side during her moment of need.

He texted Karen to let her know there had been a change of plans and asked her to meet him at the office to install the cameras so he could visit Alicia at the hospital. Karen agreed to do the installation and hoped it would give her an opportunity to do some snooping of her own.

Jonathan sat in the rental car and waited on the retired agent's arrival. He sailed in a pool of guilt as he sat in the parking lot. He thought about all of the things Alicia had done for him in the past; helping him to get on his feet and establish his dream business. Did he owe her more than what he was giving? He felt like such a hypocrite going about his life and relationships in a manner he would usually advise against when talking with his clients. How was it he had become this person? He questioned as he prepared himself for the first face-to-face with Alicia since their breakup.

Karen arrived in the parking lot. She greeted Jonathan eager to get a glimpse of his patient records. He had shared a few details about his thoughts surrounding Illuminus and Omari's murder, but she couldn't help but wonder if there was more to the story than what he was willing to share with her. She greeted Jonathan. Grabbed the duffle bag from his car and watched as he pulled off, leaving her to raid his office in peace unbeknownst to him.

Karen began accessing the inside perimeter of Jonathan's office. She placed the hidden cameras throughout the building adequately. She made her way to the main office where she placed the remainder of the cameras. Karen came upon Jonathan's file cabinet where he kept the majority of his patients' records. She began looking through the bulk of the files to locate Omari's'.

As she searched the files, she came across Elizabeth's file. It appeared to be in the wrong place. Karen took notice that the file appeared to be an assessment of Elizabeth made by a Dr. Maxwell Meadows. She scanned through the lengthy file to find anything that would give her a better understanding of Jonathan's concern for Elizabeth. Karen scanned the files and learned that Elizabeth had been a patient of Jonathan's uncle.

Since the age of six, Elizabeth had been seen for various psychosocial issues such as anxiety, depression, and insomnia. Her file detailed that her therapist concluded that she had been suffering from delusions that could have been brought on by some unknown trauma. Her file detailed that she had described being able to teleport herself into the spirit world, and other environments. With medical intervention, Elizabeth started sleeping better, having less anxiety, and eventually stopped having the delusions. By the time Elizabeth became a teenager, she was no longer suffering from the delusions or insomnia. However, her doctor noted that he felt she was not always being honest with him about her mental state in regard to her previous issues.

It was all starting to come together now. Karen was making sense of Jonathan's concerns for his friend. Elizabeth sounded like a fragile specimen that the Illuminus Society could tarnish easily if they desired. She wondered if the doctor listed could give her more details about Elizabeth.

She dialed the number listed on the files. Karen sat on the phone anxious to hear more about Elizabeth. "The Meadow's residence. How may I help you?" A voice inquired. "Hi, my name is Karen. I'm trying to reach a Doctor Maxwell Meadows. Is he in by any chance?" "Sure," the serene voice replied, placing Karen on hold.

"Hello, this is Maxwell Meadows. How can I help you?" The man asked. "Hello, Dr. Meadows. My name is Dr. Karen Black. I am calling to inquire about a new client of mine named Elizabeth Smith. I received her case file today, and I saw that you were her former therapist for a significant amount of time. I was wondering if you could tell me a little more about her."

"Yes, I remember Miss Smith. She was an interesting young lady. Her mother reached out to me when Elizabeth was around the age of five or six. She had some concerns about her mental state after she found her laid outside one night wrapped in a blanket frantically shaking. Her mother said she told her she had teleported into the spirit world where she had contact with her father. Her father died when she was three, so she never got the opportunity to forge a real relationship with him. Her mother's initial thought was that Elizabeth was acting out due to the absence of not having a father figure in her life; fabricating stories to get attention. When they first came to me, for help, I assumed the same after going through similar situations week after week with Elizabeth."

"I had installed a glass wall in the office so parents and children could feel more comfortable during our sessions. The parent and child would be able to have a visual of one another during the entire session. However, the sound would be blocked out for confidentiality purposes. One day, during one of Elizabeth's sessions, something happened. The details left me and her mother floored and concerned that we had taken the wrong approach with her. Elizabeth was sitting on the sofa in my office, and in mid-conversation, she disappeared right before our eyes. Fifteen minutes later she appeared on the sofa again."

Karen sat on the other end of the phone, listening to Dr. Meadows, feeling shocked by the details. "So, what you're saying is, you watched my client magically disappear, and then reappear in your office?" She asked to understand. "I know it sounds crazy, but I'm telling you exactly what I saw. After that incident, her mother didn't bring her back to therapy for a few weeks. A month later, she returned after she had experienced another disappearing incident. Shortly after, the visits started to dwindle and she stopped coming altogether. I tried reaching out numerous times to encourage her mother to let her come back to therapy, but she insisted they were ok and didn't need it any longer. I assumed her mother felt therapy wasn't needed after she found out Elizabeth hadn't been lying after all."

"You're telling me you believe Elizabeth could teleport into the spirit world?" Karen asked as she secretly concluded that Dr. Meadows was a quack doctor who was currently off his wagon. "I'm telling you what I saw. I don't know where she went, but I do know she disappeared before my eyes and that is a day a doctor could never forget," concluded Dr. Meadows. Karen ended the conversation feeling more intrigued to know who Elizabeth was and what the Illuminus Society wanted with her.

Did Jonathan know about Elizabeth's alleged abilities? Karen wondered. She placed Elizabeth's file back and scanned through Omari's' to see if there was any information in the file that Jonathan did not share with her, but there was nothing. Karen could hear Taylor turning her key to enter the office. She placed the files back in their rightful place, and exited the building through the back entrance as fast as she could without being spotted.

Elizabeth woke up to find Jonathan gone for the morning. The table was set with fresh fruit, waffles, and orange juice. There was a letter from Jonathan thanking her for her hospitality. Elizabeth sat at the table, consuming her breakfast when she felt a sharp surge of pain in the top of her head. She ignored the pain, writing it off as a migraine brought on by hunger, and continued eating. She reached for a spoonful of fruit when a sharp pain submerged again. This time in the back of her head. Elizabeth stood up prepared to leave the breakfast table in search of a migraine aid when she collapsed to the floor. She hit her head on the edge of the table on the way down. Elizabeth lay still on the floor completely blacked out.

A few minutes later, she found herself in a dark environment she had never seen before. Elizabeth looked around the dark black space to make out any adjacent image she could find, but there was none. She yelled for assistance, but no one came. Elizabeth's anxiety started to elevate quickly. It left her flustered and frightened as she stood in the middle of the pitch black room confused, trying to understand where she was and how she had gotten there.

A light emerged in the center of the room. It revealed a picture image similar to a movie from a projector. Elizabeth approached the image. She was confused as a sound began to emerge louder and louder. On the screen, a college ballplayer was running with a ball. The player appeared to be exiting a game where he was approached by a disfigured short man. The image showed the ballplayer and the man talking. The man handed the player a crest shaped pin.

As the movie image continued to play, Elizabeth could see that the young man had aged some. The next image showed the ballplayer at what appeared to be a ceremony. The room was filled with people wearing red hoods and their faces were not visible. A young child approached the center of the room, holding a dagger as a cage with a goat inside began to emerge from the center of the floor. The child approached the hooded adults who were all lined up in the center of the room. The child slit the goat's middle section, and each adult held out their hands and allowed the small child to slit the center of their palms with the dagger. The child combined the blood of the goat with the blood in the center of each person's hand.

Elizabeth listened as a hooded woman began to talk, who sat at the forefront of the room. She placed a significance on the blood ritual. She expressed that the blood of the goat mixing with the human blood was symbolic for each individual. The woman explained that each person would leave the room transformed into a goat of success in their individual career realms.

The room went completely dark. There was no longer a projection of images on the wall. Elizabeth started to feel fearful. She teleported into another environment within seconds. She looked around feeling more frightened than she did before, as she stood in the middle of an unfamiliar graveyard. She scanned the area to find a familiar indicator of where she was and why. But, there was nothing but tombstones present. There was a stiff cold mist of fog rolling through the atmosphere.

She heard a noise and looked up to find a man in a red hooded robe that appeared to be the same robe from the projected images. She started to shiver as the man approached her in complete silence. Fear compiled in the top portion of her chest as her heart began to beat faster and faster. The man pulled off his hood and exposed his face which appeared to be discolored. "Are you okay," Elizabeth asked as her voice rattled with fear. The man stood still not uttering a word.

"Can I help you?" She asked this time feeling a bigger rush of anxiety as the man lifted his head and made eye contact with her. "We need your help," he said in a dim tone. He dropped his head again as if he were a zombie. "Who's we?" She asked with a trembling present in her voice. Elizabeth looked up to find the graveyard filled with people standing adjacent to tombstones wearing the same red hooded robe as the discolored man.

"They are coming for you, too," the man said while keeping his head slumped in a downward position. Before Elizabeth could open her mouth to inquire what he was referencing, he continued with a more miscellaneous dialect. "She put us here. Find her and you will have all the answers," he said, placing his hood back over his head. Elizabeth looked up in shock as she watched the hooded crowd disappear before her eyes.

The discolored man turned and began walking away. "Wait? I don't understand!" She yelled out to get the man's attention. His head detached from his body and he held it in his hands as he walked closer and closer to his tombstone before disappearing completely. Elizabeth stood in the graveyard frozen from shock. She couldn't believe what she had witnessed.

The area went black again and there was nothing in sight. "Elizabeth, Elizabeth!" A loud voice called to her. She felt someone tugging on her body vigorously to get her to come to. She began to come around, opening her eyes to find Jonathan hovering over her. "Are you okay?" He asked. She began to sit up slowly. She felt a thumping pain on the side of her head. She held the area of her head in hopes to overpower the throbbing with her hand and removed it to find her fingers covered in blood.

"What happened?" She asked as she sat up on the floor. "I don't know. I came in and found you passed out on the floor. It looks like you hit your head on the edge of the table," he explained as he assessed the blood on her head and fingers. "Wait here while I get you cleaned up," Jonathan instructed. Elizabeth did as she was told. She sat in the middle of the floor as she tried to fight off the dizzy sensation. Jonathan rushed back to her side. He kneeled down on the floor and cleaned her head injury ridding it of the blood.

"What happened?" he asked. "I'm not sure," she said, still trying to wrap her mind around it all. "I remember watching a weird movie, then I was in a graveyard and I was approached by this man wearing a red robe. The man told me to find her." "Who's her?" asked Jonathan. "I don't know. When I tried to find out who and what he was referring to, he turned and walked away. He was holding his head." "His head?" Jonathan asked. He tried to make sense of what she was telling him. "Maybe I hit my head too hard," Elizabeth said as she tried to ease her way up off of the floor slowly, with her head still spinning and throbbing at the injury site. Jonathan listened as Elizabeth explained what she thought was a dream. However, he knew otherwise.

He thought about her file information and how his uncle Maxwell had informed him of Elizabeth's ability early on in their friendship. His uncle breached his confidentiality agreement with her as his client. Maxwell had informed Jonathan of her ability to project and teleport between the spirit world and the human world in hopes to give Elizabeth an ally and a protector if she ever needed one.

Jonathan didn't know what to do. He cared deeply for his friend, and he had always felt like she had been shielded from her truth for far too long. What he didn't understand was how it was that Elizabeth had somehow forgotten her ability. So he took a leap of faith at that moment and decided to do what he felt was right and inform her of her truth.

Jonathan helped Elizabeth to her bedroom to get positioned in the bed comfortably before unloading on her. She laid there deep in thought as she recalled the discolored man's face and the hooded crowd huddled alongside tombstones in the graveyard. "Are you feeling okay?" he asked as he took notice of Elizabeth's spaced-out demeanor. "I'm ok. I just keep thinking about the weird dream I had," she replied.

"I need to talk to you about something," Jonathan said hesitantly. "There's something I think you need to know." Elizabeth sat up in the bed and took notice of the serious look that had taken over Jonathan's face within seconds. "Do you remember the therapist you used to see as a child?" he asked. "Vaguely why?" She asked, not understanding what he was getting at. "Years after you stopped therapy he reached out to me. During that time, I was in my final semester of school. Your therapist was my mother's oldest brother, Maxwell." "Yes, and," Elizabeth stated as she tried to figure out where Jonathan was headed.

"Well, Maxwell reached out to me asking that I keep a close eye on you. He told me you had been having some troubles, and he was worried about you. When I asked him what kind of trouble he neglected to tell me the specifics. He stated that he could not do so because of confidentiality reasons. Once I became an official doctor of psychiatry, my uncle reached out again. We had a brief conversation and a few minutes later I received a fax from him. The fax included a detailed file with all of your information in it from the time you had spent under his care.

Elizabeth sat on the bed with a puzzled look on her face. She attempted to understand what could have been so important that her therapist would decide to break his confidentiality agreement with her to inform her best friend of the details of their time together. "I'm sorry Jonathan, but that time period of my life is really a blur. Honestly, I don't even remember why I started seeing a therapist in the first place.

Jonathan hated being the bringer of bad news and bad memories. And, it was clear to him that he was about to open a can of worms Elizabeth had no recollection of. "According to my uncle, your mother sought out his help after she found you outside shivering in the cold in the middle of the night. At first glance, she assumed you had been sleepwalking and she wrote it off as nothing. However, a few days later it happened again. When she asked you what happened, your mother told my uncle that you had told her a detailed story that was disturbing and she assumed it was a cry for attention.

"What was the story?" Elizabeth asked. Jonathan hesitated to answer. "Well, what was it?" She asked again. "Your mother said you told her you had traveled to the spirit world, and while you were there you visited with your father." Elizabeth sat still and held off on a response.

Memories started rushing to her mind, making the throbbing sensation worse. She tried to stand, grabbing her temple on each side, hoping to stop the rush of memories, but they continued to come. She was rendered helpless as she fell to the ground unable to stop the pain or the memories from re-implanting themselves in her brain. Jonathan rushed to her aide and tried to understand what was happening, as he watched Elizabeth scream. She held her temple and curled up in a fetal position on the floor.

He felt a surge of guilt take over realizing that giving her the truth may not have been the best idea. The screams stopped and the room went silent. Jonathan looked around the room and saw nothing but pitch black. He could feel Elizabeth still balled up on the floor beside him. "What's happening?" She asked as her body continued to shiver. "You need to control it. It's your gift, but you have to learn to control it," Jonathan encouraged.

Before Elizabeth could respond, their surroundings changed. Elizabeth lifted her head slowly and assessed the beautiful, serene surroundings that had emerged out of nowhere. The grass was the greenest grass she had ever seen, and the trees were tall, all filled with birds, and butterflies. The air smelled fresh and calm as if it had never been polluted with a single toxin. Elizabeth felt stunned as she took notice of the beautiful brown-skinned woman approaching her in an all-white gown that blew in the same direction as the wind, with her head full of thick locs spiraled up into a bun.

It was as if they had somehow stepped into the most beautiful dream of all time. Jonathan stood in the grass adjacent to Elizabeth. He helped Elizabeth to stand. When he looked up, he become in sync with Elizabeth as they both glared at the beautiful woman with surprise. "Hello, Jonathan. I see you are still quite the gentleman I remember," the woman said. She gained no response as Jonathan stared at her in complete shock. He was unable to forge a single sentence in response to the woman's compliment. "Hello, beautiful daughter," the woman said to Elizabeth as she wiped the tears from her eyes. "No need for tears," she assured. "I don't understand. I thought you were…you're supposed to be…" Elizabeth stammered struggling to finish her sentence.

"I am," the woman replied, holding the most beautiful serene smile Elizabeth had ever seen. "I am here to help you. You are about to enter a pivotal time in your life, and you will need to rely on your gifts now more than ever. To do that, you will need to believe in yourself. Believe that you can control your abilities and you will. Believe that they will control you, and they will," the woman said as she wiped away the final tear flowing down Elizabeth's face. Elizabeth looked away and when she turned to question the specifics of her mother's choice of words, she had disappeared, and she and Jonathan were back in her apartment lying on the floor of her bedroom. Jonathan stood up quickly and helped Elizabeth off the floor. He didn't know what to say.

He had started the conversation to tell Elizabeth the truth about her past she had conveniently forgotten, then just like that she had stepped into her past dragging him along for the ride. He wanted to console her with words as he caressed her back while she lay on his chest sobbing uncontrollably, but the right words never came to mind. "All this time she could help me see her, talk to her, touch her and she did nothing. Nothing," she repeated as her cries became louder. "Why would she do that?" Elizabeth asked rhetorically.

"I don't know, but there has to have been a reason for it. I'm sure," Jonathan replied. "Your mother was one of the sweetest, most caring people I ever had the opportunity of knowing. I don't know why she waited so long to show herself to you. But, I do know there has to be a good reason. She would never do anything to hurt you. Maybe, it's something you did or didn't do. You shut out memory of your abilities, maybe you had to be vulnerable for her to be able to communicate."

"Vulnerable? I've been vulnerable for months. Losing a parent has that effect on you." She replied aggressively. She was frustrated by Jonathan's response. Elizabeth knew he was only trying to help, but she didn't think he was making much sense. How could he insinuate that she had not previously been vulnerable? "I'm sorry," he said. "I didn't mean it in that way. All I was trying to say is maybe your mother was waiting for the perfect moment." He attempted to clear up his previous statement that even he felt was idiotic.

"What did she mean by a pivotal time in my life?" Elizabeth asked.

Jonathan wanted to mention the fact that in less than two hours she was going to be going through the induction process for a secret society he now believed to be deadly and dangerous, but he said nothing. He tucked Elizabeth back in bed and urged her to rest until it was time for her to prepare for the ceremony.

He departed the bedroom filled with worry for his friend. He had witnessed her abilities up close and personal, and was now more sure than ever that Elizabeth had been selected by Illuminus for a lot more than she was aware of. He started to wonder if Omari had exhibited any abilities similar to the ones he now knew for certain Elizabeth possessed. Jonathan remembered Omari listed his mother's information in his files for his emergency contact reference. Jonathan rushed to his rental car and headed to his office to retrieve what he needed in hopes he could find a solid piece of evidence he could present to Elizabeth before the induction to keep her from making a huge mistake.

Queen Mother stood in the mirror glancing at her face that didn't look a day over thirty. Yet, she somehow managed to feel discontent anytime she saw herself in the mirror. She would find a flaw that no one else could see existed. She had been the leader of the Illuminus Society for quite some time. She took over the reins as the matriarch that everyone wanted to know more about.

She lived a double life, and hid her true identity from all except Magnus, her trusted loyal sidekick. She pretended to be a timid stay-at-home mom when roaming out into the regular world. But, in reality, timid and invisible was something she could never truly be. She hated going home to her husband and family life, having to play a role she could never really encompass; pretending to be a wife, mom, and and an irrelevant factor to most who crossed her path. She hated going along with whatever her husband wanted, allowing him to make the rules, make the money, and run the household while she stood in the shadows seeming to be of no significance to anyone other than her children. She silently dreamed about the day she would have the opportunity to have power in the world. She wanted to be identified as something more than her title as a mom and wife.

Tonight was more than just a ceremony to recruit new members for the Queen Mother. It would also be the night she would have the opportunity to invite her youngest-born child into her life. From the outside looking in, Giselle appeared to have many of her qualities. She was beautiful, ambitious, and intelligent. Queen Mother had spent several weeks watching and having others watch Giselle. They would report full details to her such as where Giselle ate, when, and what, never having spared a detail in hopes to get to know the child she had left behind.

She thought about Giselle every day, wondering what she was like. She had been waiting patiently for the day she could offer her a seat at the table of Illuminus. One of the promises she had made to Sam before his death was to preserve and use his sperm to create a child that could carry out the legacy of Illuminus, once he was no longer present to do so.

Queen Mother thought about her last days with Sam, holding on to the moments they shared. This plagued her return home to her husband and children every day for years. She saw so much of Sam's presence in Giselle; in her eyes, smile, and her overall will to do whatever she needed to do to reach her goals. For it was in these details alone that the Queen Mother found assurance that Sam's genetics combined with hers had created the perfect human specimen.

She hated living a double life, feeling the freedom of strength running through her veins each day she spoke to her followers through the speakers of the Illuminus mansion. She struggled to appreciate the humility she experienced when arriving home to make dinner, do laundry, and listen to her wealthy husband discuss politics and business in front of her as if he felt she could never truly relate, because her life consisted of nothing meaningful in his eyes.

Queen Mother hated walking out of her position of power and walking into the normal space she held in her family life. Lately, her husband had been gaining more and more business contacts and more and more deposits. This left him swamped with more work, less time for her, and less care for her mental state. To him, a paycheck increase was the key to all of life's problems. Bigger checks meant better meals, better homes, better trips, and a better lifestyle in his eyes. Little did he know the more money he made the more problems his wife was experiencing due to his lack of presence and consistency in their marriage.

She desired more than designer shoes and bags, or the occasional trip out of the country. The things she desired were things money could not buy. She couldn't bring herself to understand why men in powerful prestigious positions always felt like a wife that was wined and dined with money and material items was happy. For, in reality, she was anything but happy in her marriage and home life.

Being at the forefront of all things, Illuminus gave her a stature she had never witnessed any woman have. The culture of life she came from had always taught her that this is a man's world and she was desperate to change that narrative. Sam had given her detailed instructions surrounding how Illuminus should be conducted, but due to her own endeavors, she had decided that not many of his instructions were conducive to the future she had envisioned for the society. She hated betraying Sam's trust, but she had no choice. In her mind, he had been doing things improperly for years and there was no real gain without sacrifice. So, she sacrificed their trust among many other things in hopes to achieve a higher outcome for Illuminus than what Sam ever could.

Queen Mother had never loved any man the way she loved Sam. She constantly took in deep stares and observations of her current husband. She was annoyed by the fact that he could never measure up to be half the man Sam was. Feeling plagued by loneliness every long night her husband worked, hating the sight of Gucci, Fendi, and Prada, wanting her love to be wrapped in simplicity, daydreaming about receiving an "I miss you" text or a simple date night that didn't require an expensive tab alongside her body being wrapped inexpensive fabric. Queen Mother had become drained from being patient. She was tired of waiting on a man to learn her love language that had no desire to do so. His focus revolved around new contracts, new business opportunities, and new deposits. This left her to deduce that in her world more money only meant more problems.

Giselle stood in the mirror and looked at her dress, assessing every corner to conclude if it was the perfect dress or if she needed to change. She looked at her lace, admiring Tamra's work. She reminisced on the old dynamic they used to have days ago before she had received the money. She had been thinking about Tamra ever since she left Alicia's house. She wondered what she could do to make things right between the two of them. Often having to suppress the urge to pick up the phone and call, realizing that over the years she was only able to make amends with Tamra when she initiated the apology. She was tired of doing that in situations where she did not feel she was the one in the wrong. What was it that made an apology so hard for Tamra? Why did she always have to be so stubborn and entitled? She wondered.

As Giselle became consumed with thoughts of her and Tamra's spat, she heard a loud knock at the door. She walked to the door and glanced through the peephole. Stunned to find Lamont on the other side of the door, she debated if she should open the door for him or ignore him and hope for his departure. "I know you're in there, Giselle," he said, conveying to her that he would not be going anywhere until she opened the door. "What do you want, Lamont?" She asked, well aware that it was closure he had come to her front door in search of.

Giselle had managed to avoid Lamont every day after the alarming kiss. She was having mixed feelings about it. "Please just open the door and talk to me face to face like a normal civilized person," he said, making it extremely difficult for her to turn him down. Giselle opened the door quickly making it clear to Lamont she was not happy to see him. "Civilized!" she yelled. "How dare you talk to me about being civilized when you're the one who kissed me, knowing you're in a relationship with my cousin!" She glanced into the hall, and took notice of a nosey neighbor with a shocked look on her face and slammed the door abruptly. "I can't believe you. Tamra is one of the most important people in the world to me and I would never want to do anything to hurt her," Giselle cried out.

"I know," he said, rushing over to console her as he looked around the room enthralled by Giselle's choice of decor. Everything about her made him feel like she was someone to keep close. He couldn't explain it. He had spent his entire life gaining the reputation of being a playboy, yet, one close look at Giselle made him want to be someone different. He held her close while he tried to make her feel safe with him. He secretly wished he could go back in time and clear his reputation of all the things that would plague a woman like Giselle to want to steer clear of him, but he could not. He knew it was wrong to try and seek out the attention of Tamra's cousin and friend, but he felt little guilt due to the circumstances of his and Tamra's relationship.

He wanted to open up to Giselle and tell her that her cousin was in fact not the person she thought she was. He wanted to tell her all the stories he had where Tamra had caused him the same hurt she so freely addressed in reference to him. He wanted to tell Giselle about all the sidebar conversations he overheard Tamra having on the phone with others about her, but he knew his attempts would be deciphered as self-motivated. So, he held her while she cried expressing how she felt something when they kissed that she had never felt before.

She wanted to walk away from the entire experience while feeling something nudging her in Lamont's direction against her will. She got her emotions together accepting the Kleenex from Lamont. Every time she was in his presence, it wiped away all the residue of the fear she felt in relation to intimacy. Lamont took a step back, noticing Giselle's attire. He wondered where she could be going in such a formal dress.

"Where are you going?" he asked, anticipating her answer. He thought a dress like the one she was wearing usually came with a male hanging on to her arm accompanying her to a date. "I have an event, or at least I'm supposed to," she said, glancing at her phone anticipating a message from Illuminus with the details of when and where to arrive. "Do you need a date," he asked with a sneaky smirk on his face. He attempted to slide in with Giselle in any way he could.

"No," she said, annoyed that Lamonts only focus was still the status of their relationship. "Well, can I at least give you a ride to where you're going?" Giselle wanted to accept Lamonts offer in hopes she wouldn't cross paths with Mia again, but she knew that was not an option. She booked an Uber and allowed Lamont to get out the last of his feelings before she sent him on his way "Where do we go from here?" He asked, feeling like they had not reached much of a conclusion during their conversation. Giselle didn't know what to say. She hated being in such a compromising situation. She knew in less than an hour she would be inducted into Illuminus, and her life would change forever, so for now she felt it was best to be inconspicuous when it came to Lamont until she got things figured out.

Lamont made his exit from the upscale condo-style apartment. She sensed he did not receive what he had come there for which was an indefinite response to how they should move forward after the kiss.

13

The Induction

Giselle took one last glance in the mirror, assessing her attire. Her anxiety had peaked since Lamont's surprise visit. The time had approached closer for the induction ceremony. She kept thinking about her conversation with Christophe, and the unexpected lump sum that had appeared in her bank account. The closer she came to becoming an official member of Illuminus, the more she started to worry.

Giselle knew she needed to break her stressful thoughts. She booked an Uber so she wouldn't be late. She then heard a knock at the door. She dreaded the thought of seeing Lamont again, after their awkward conversation.

She opened the door abruptly, expecting it to be him. To her surprise, it was a delivery man, wearing an Illuminus crest at the top right pocket corner of his uniform. "Ma'am, I have a delivery for a Giselle Howard," he said with a smile on his face. "That's me," she replied, She was confused as to what it was that could be delivered to her at such a strange hour. "Can you sign here?" The man asked as he handed her the signature form, still appearing to be extremely happy in an awkward way.

Giselle signed the form and handed it back to the delivery man. He turned and rushed away from the door. "Wait a minute," she said. "You didn't give me my package." The man looked at her with a grin, "I'm afraid it's a little too heavy to transport to your front door, but it's waiting outside for you," he said, still smiling as he rushed away. "Well, if it's too heavy for you then how the heck do you think I'm supposed to be able to get it upstairs…Idiot," she said under her breath as she walked down the stairs of her building to approach the front door.

She looked out of the door confused to find that there was no package there. She walked outside to check the parameter. She noticed a black Lamborghini parked out front with a gigantic bow plastered on top. Surely this could not be the gift the delivery man was referring to. Giselle approached the vehicle where she found a small envelope with the Illuminus crest stamped on top. She opened the envelope and found a note that read,

Dear Giselle,

I'm sure you're shocked by all the blessings that have been coming your way in such a short period of time. It's all so confusing, but I hope in due time it will all make sense. We have a lot of catching up to do and my hope is that I can make up for all the lost time. There is so much I need and want to tell you. There is also so much I hope and pray that you will be able to forgive me for. But, in due time we will be reunited. I look forward to seeing you at the ceremony tonight.

Giselle was more confused now than ever. She read over the note several times. She wanted to make sense of it. First the money, then the luxury vehicle, and then the letter. She pinpointed the author's choice of words. She focused on keywords, "forgiveness" and "reunion." What did the author mean by reunited? And, what was there that needed to be forgiven?

As she began to ponder and fall into another thoughtful state, her phone went off and a message came across her screen. It gave her the location of the induction ceremony. She had twenty minutes to make a timely arrival.

Giselle hopped into her new vehicle and headed to the ceremony, now more anxious and concerned than ever. Christophe had tried his best to prepare her for the ceremony. She was starting to wonder if maybe he had left out some key details of why she had been selected. She had no clue who it was that she would be reuniting with, but she was on her way to find out, prepared for anything that came her way.

Queen Mother started to feel anxious after not hearing from Magnus in a timely fashion. Had he failed to recruit Alicia as she requested? Before she could question his results any further, she received a text informing her that he had arrived in the main room to complete the setup along with Alicia. Queen Mother sat at her table determined to get her thoughts together before the ceremony.

She wondered if she had made the right choice bringing Giselle back into her life after such an elongated departure. How was she going to explain her lack of mothering? What would Giselle think of her, after hearing her selfish motives as to why she had abandoned her? Most importantly would she be forgiven?

Queen Mother quickly rejected all of the negative questions that were rolling around in her mind. She turned her attention to the ceremony. Tonight would be the start of a new chapter in the cultivation of Illuminus. She had no time to ponder on the negative possibilities when there was much work that needed to be done.

She rose from her seat, walked towards the mirror, and pushed in the top right corner, exposing a hidden door and walkway. She made her way through the dark walkway, setting off motion censored lights that were embedded in the walls.

Queen Mother came upon a giant altar. Several colorful candles were aligned on the top of the mantle along with a cross covered in blood, severed phalanges, and a beaker filled with filtered animal secretions. She began lighting the candles one by one as she picked up the severed finger bones chanting repetitively "L'excellence noire est L'avenir" (Black excellence is the future in French). She placed the bones back on top of the altar and picked up the beaker of blood. She spread the contents over the candles and the fingerbones, as she continued chanting faster and faster. She waited for a sign from her ancestors that the chant had penetrated its way through to the spirit world, as she called forth for help from the dead. She wanted to make tonight a night that all of the inductees would remember. She waited by the altar for Sam to show himself to her, waiting for a sign that his spirit was in the room, but there was nothing.

She felt consumed with worry right away. She had conducted the same blood ceremony year after year, conjuring up communication from her dead loved one. Yet, this time she received no definite response from Sam. This lead her to wonder if she had done something improperly to prolong his return. She blew out the candles and departed from the hidden ritual room immediately with no results.

The absence of Sam appearance lead her to fear that she did not have his blessing to move forward with the ceremony as she had in the past. She could not risk canceling and missing out on the opportunity to meet her long-lost daughter, or the opportunity to rear the society in a new direction that permitted growth and elevation on a level that even Sam himself was unable to cultivate. So, she did what she felt was well warranted and moved forward despite her lack of communication from the spirits.

Magnus put on his red robe and glared at his disfigured image in the mirror. He had been a part of several ceremonies, but he could feel the differentiation of significance as the anticipation of the ceremony rose to its peak. He often thought about his former life of struggle and abandonment. He was full of gratitude regarding the current life he had because of Queen Mother. He knew letting her down would be the last thing in the world he would ever want to do. He pulled the hood over his head, as he exited his office, making his way towards the ceremony room. He entered the dark room and calmly awaited the arrival of the others.

Moments later, a long line of robed individuals entered in. They lined up silently, with hoods covering their heads, making it impossible to make out clear visual indicators of who they were. Queen Mother sat at the forefront of the room dressed in an eccentric crimson red catsuit that had an opulent face covering. It clung to her, shielding her face from anything and everything besides the particles of oxygen that filled the room. General Silver entered the room with a line of Illuminus troops. He was accompanied by the soon-to-be inducted members; Elizabeth, Giselle, Thomas, Jackson, Gabriella, Idris, Lamar, Karen, and Alicia. They all entered the room filled with anxiety.

The wall-mounted candles began to flicker boisterously in the distance as the Queen Mother rose from her seat. "I am honored to have you all here this evening," she said, looking at the group of men and women as they took in the imagery of their surroundings. The inductees wondered if she was going to reveal her face. She began to inform them of their path and purpose with the society. She spoke to them about their futures as she touched lightly on why they were selected. Queen Mother highlighted the significance of being chosen to be a part of the secret society. She glorified black excellence and the future of the World of Illuminus, and reiterated over and over how fortunate they were to have been selected.

"Is it just me or is her fit screaming met Gala Seance?" Elizabeth whispered in Giselle's ear, forcing her to chuckle against her will.

Silver glared over at the two young women and gave them an evil stare as Queen Mother continued her spill. Giselle leaned over to Elizabeth. "She definitely would give the Kar-Jenners and Riri a run for their money," Giselle said, sparking a smirk from Elizabeth. "I'm Giselle by the way," she whispered. "Hi, Giselle. I'm Elizabeth," she whispered in response. "So, what brings you here," Elizabeth murmured. "Honestly, I am still trying to figure that out," Giselle whispered to her new acquaintance.

Queen Mother sat in her seat. The room became completely dark and still. Giselle grabbed Elizabeth's arm frightened by the abrupt darkness. The candles emerged again and the inductees could see that the chair that once held the mysterious speaker was now empty.

"Sorry," Giselle said quickly, freeing Elizabeth's arm from bondage. "It's okay. This is giving creepy vibes. I'm starting to question why I'm here, too. But, I guess it beats standing in the unemployment line," said Elizabeth. "I'm not so sure," Giselle responded as she stood in fear along with the other inductees, waiting for whatever it was that was going to come their way next.

The whole experience reminded Giselle of the traumatizing and dehumanizing ritual the sorority she tried to join had put her through. However, she knew that leaving wouldn't be as easy of a task. For if she even thought about it, consequences would be dire, and getting away would be nothing more than a pipe dream.

Magnus took to the center of the room, announcing that the ceremony was now in commencement. The lights departed again and left the room darker than before. Giselle and Elizabeth grabbed a hold of one another. This time in unison. Both feared what was to come.

Two minutes later, the dim lighting was back and Magnus was gone. "What in the black Houdini is going on here?" Questioned Elizabeth to Giselle in a whisper tone. "Girl, I don't have a clue? Because, last I checked, black people don't do settings like this."

A midsized cage started to emerge from the center of the floor. Both girls were silent as they heard the goat noises coming from the cage. A small, hooded child started approaching the cage in the center of the room. She had been handed a dagger by one of the red hooded individuals in the room. The little girl approached the cage, watching as the cage corners depleted, leaving the goat in the center of the room with the cage barriers no longer intact.

The small girl continued walking towards the goat, with the dagger prepared to go through with the bloodletting ritual, when the room went completely dark again. This time alarming the small child holding the dagger as she screamed to the top of her lungs out of fear of surprise due to the unanticipated blackout.

"Get the lights!" Silver screamed to his troops. As they all ran to follow through with his orders, the lights came on without any intervention. In the center of the room was a head sitting on the podium adjacent to the cageless goat. The little girl ran over to the inductees, grabbing hold of Giselle as she closed her eyes, crying out in fear. "It's okay," Giselle said, rubbing her back to calm the small child despite the fear that was running through her veins.

"What in the name of Lord Voldemort were they going to have her do with that dagger," Elizabeth whispered to Giselle as she watched the lighting reemerge and cut off again. The little girl grabbed Giselle tighter, still squeezing her eyes shut afraid of the dark room. The lights returned, alarming the room as everyone watched the head that sat on the podium begin to rise from its resting place.

It floated through the air until it exploded into pieces, plastering the contents all over the podium and the surrounding area. A man stood in the middle of the room, bringing General Silver's bottom lip to the floor as he watched the event unfold in disbelief. As the man stood in the center of the room, he noticed the troops ready to act on his arrival. Kyle withdrew his red hood from his head ready to approach the man, but he was signaled to stay in position by General Silver.

Giselle recognized the friendly Uber driver's face as she assessed the unfolding in the middle of the room. "What is Illuminus?" The man asked as he looked around the room. He focused the bulk of his attention on the group of newbies that stood confused before his eyes. "They will tell you it is a one-way ticket into the realm of success. They will inform you that after being inducted you will become a goat of success," he continued. "Some of you may be wondering why the beautiful little girl, approaching the goat was holding a dagger. Illuminus was going to have her sacrifice the goat, mixing its blood with a small portion of yours. Traumatic I know! They want to convince you that this particular ritual would be the necessary resource to turn you all into goats of success, fast-tracking you on the road to black excellence. They would have you believe that Illuminus is the sun and the moon, and you all are privileged to be a part of something as spectacular as this well-renowned society. But, I am here to give you the truth."

Giselle's eyes and ears opened wide as she watched the intriguing man speak of knowing truths about the intricate society. "Like you all,

I stood in this very room years ago, awaiting my turn to be inducted into what I thought would be a life-changing opportunity. I made it through the ceremony, and that same day my life changed forever. I received a professional contract to play ball, millions of dollars, endorsements, and the list goes on. What I didn't know is to whom much is given much is required. I would soon be required to take part in treacherous acts I never wanted to be a part of. Doing whatever I was told to do to help keep their secrets."

"I hurt people's livelihood, exposing teammates who no longer wanted to be a part of the organization, and ruptured families in hopes to keep Illuminus happy and secure. I played their game until my conscience would no longer allow me to play anymore and you know what happened?" The room stood still as the man looked around waiting for an answer. "I said do you know what happened?!" He yelled aggressively. "I ended up getting my head cut off," he said as his head detached from his body, dropping into his hands like a modern-day African-American version of the headless horseman.

Everyone began screaming, running towards the door in fear. Giselle grabbed the little girl, picking her up and holding her tightly while charging for the exit. As they ran, all of the entrances in the room slammed loudly, alarming the entire room as they heard the bolts lock into place. "People, people, please just calm down," the headless man said. "There's nothing to be afraid of. I'm not here to hurt you. I'm here to warn you so you don't end up like me," he said, placing his head back into its place. "I admit that was a little over the top, but let's just say death has made me a little more pessimistic than what I'd prefer to be," the man said as he rose to the ceiling making his way over to the two women and small child.

"Well, well, well, this is very interesting," the man said as he took notice of the small girl wrapped in Giselle's arms. "I have to admit, black love is a very very complex thing. Boy meets girl. Boy and girl fall in love, and then boy and girl have children. The boy dies, the children are separated and given up at birth. And before you know it, the children are reunited during an induction ceremony," the cryptic ghost continued as he hovered his way around the room over to the hooded individuals.

"Was he trying to say…?" Elizabeth started to ask before cutting herself off. She hadn't witnessed this much drama in one room since her last binge of reality T.V. She didn't know what to make of the messy ghost, flying overhead. But, she was certain that the Illuminus Society was offering a lot more during the commencement than what they had initially intended to.

Kyle stared at Giselle and the small girl, wondering if the maliciousness the ghost was spreading was true. Could it be possible that he and Giselle were not the only children abandoned by their mother? Was the little girl in fact a blood relative? And if so, were there others? His head was spinning. He couldn't believe what he was seeing or hearing as he looked at the little girl. He noticed how she and Giselle were the spitting image of one another.

The ghost hovered overhead for minutes before pulling the red hood from one of the hooded men, revealing Jonathan's face. This alarmed Elizabeth and Karen right away as they both took notice of the intruder. "What's up Doc?" The ghost asked as Jonathan stood silently in shock as he watched his former dead patient taunt him and the others in the room. "I've been meaning to make my way over to talk with you. Therapy was very helpful to me, and I'm starting to find that even in death I'm a little distressed," Omari said, still hovering his way around the room.

He made his way over to General Silver. "Well Silver, it looks like your men are not so great after all. I guess Doctor Jonathan Meadows creeping his way in here like he's one of the hardy boys is proof of that! Tell your boys to tighten up," the passive-aggressive ghost whispered as he disappeared into thin air. He left the room with questions as everyone began making their way to the doors desperate to exit the induction room.

"Stop!" The aggressive voice demanded over the loudspeaker as everyone ran towards the exit, and the room continued to flood with chaos and fear. "Hold your positions and calm down immediately," the woman instructed. Everyone froze in their places. They recognized the Queen Mother's voice. They awaited further instruction. "Kyle, lead everyone to the dining area where there will be dinner and drinks for all of our guests, as well as an explanation as to what happened here tonight," she said. "Silver, bring the doctor to me," she said with a sharp tone before the speaker went completely silent.

Kyle led the room full of people to the dining room. He took notice of everyone's fearful demeanor. How could anyone consume food after what they all had just witnessed? He watched as Giselle and all of the other inductees took a seat at the same table. He assessed the looks on their faces and wondered who amongst the group was now regretting their choice to join the society.

The little girl sat at the table with the inductees, shivering as fear continued to roam through her body. "Are you ok?" Giselle asked. "No," the little girl responded anxiously. "I…I…I've never seen a real ghost before today." "What's your name?" Giselle asked. "My name is Madison. But, my friends call me Maddy." "How old are you?" Giselle asked. "I'm seven," the little girl replied. "Well, it's nice to meet you, Maddy. I'm Giselle.

Giselle couldn't bring herself to stop staring at the seven year old. It was as if she were looking in a mirror at her childhood reflection. She thought about the ghost and the accusations he had dished out subliminally. Was it possible Madison was her sister? She thought about her mother and the type of woman she was. She realized there was no way her mother would have ever had a love child and left her out in the world to fend for herself with strangers.

"Maddy, where are your parents?" Giselle inquired. "I don't know. I've been living in this house since I can remember. I have been raised by the nuns that run the nursery, like all of the other children at Illuminus mansion." "Nuns? Children? What children?" Elizabeth asked, interrupting Giselle's questions ready to ask a few of her own. "There aren't a lot of us. But, the few of us that are here, live in the nursery wing where we are cared for by the nuns that live in that part of the house," Maddy replied. She did not understand the shocked looks on the women's faces. She thought it was normal to be raised by nuns, because it was all she had ever known.

"Do these children have parents? Or is everyone under the care of the nuns alone?" asked Elizabeth. "Everyone has parents, and most of those parents live here permanently. I am the only child who doesn't have parents," said Maddy. "Why don't you have parents?" asked

Giselle. "I'm not sure. I just know that I've been here since birth. I was told that my mother was very ill and had to go away after giving birth to me. I've never met my father and no one here seems to know much about him," Maddy detailed.

Elizabeth glanced at Giselle, making eye contact to communicate nonverbally so she would not alarm the seven year old. "I feel better now," said Maddy. "Good, Would you like to go get yourself some food?" Giselle asked. "Yes, but, promise me you will be here when I get back," Maddy replied. "You have my word," Giselle said, giving the small girl a smile as she watched her walk towards the refreshments table.

"Who in the world would leave their child in a place like this?" Elizabeth asked. "I don't know what's going on here, but something isn't right. I felt it the moment I received the money, and then again when I walked through the front door." "Money? You received the money, too?" Giselle asked. She was surprised to find that she was not the only person who had received the lump sum.

"What do you think they want with us?" Giselle questioned. "I don't know, but I'm ready to take my unemployed ass back home where I came from. I didn't sign up for additional stress, orphan children, and headless ghosts. All of a sudden the World and Trust Bank and my racist ass co-workers are starting to look like my distant family members showing up to Thanksgiving...very doable!" Elizabeth replied.

Giselle had no clue what it was Elizabeth was referencing, but she knew she agreed that maybe they had bitten off more than they could chew.

"You and Maddy have a strong resemblance," Elizabeth said, letting the cat out of the bag despite the fact that she knew it was probably not the time or the place. "We do, don't we," said Giselle, still eyeing the seven year old as she watched her fill her plates with goodies from the refreshment table.

Maddy sat at the table beside Giselle. She had an unspoken level of comfort and familiarity with her. She paid attention to how Giselle's facial features were symmetrical to her own. "You look like me," Maddy said to Giselle with a mouth full of cookies as she chewed aggressively as if she was sitting down to have her first meal of the day. "It would appear that I do," Giselle said with a smile as she continued to stare at the small child. She wondered why they looked so much alike. She told herself it was mere coincidence while her intuitive nature told her it was something more.

"I hate to interrupt," a woman said, kneeling at Elizabeth's side. "I need you to come with me," said Karen. "Jonathan did not make it back to the dining room, and I think he's been captured for sneaking in." "Captured? What do you mean he's been captured?" Asked Elizabeth. "I mean just what I said," he's been captured. "And, I need you to come with me so we can go find him. I'm coming too," Giselle said. "Yassss, new friend come through!" Elizabeth said as she began to go into fight or flight mode; happy she had made a new acquaintance amongst all the chaos.

"I'm coming, too," a smaller voice replied. Giselle looked at Maddy, finding it impossible to turn her away. "I promised her I wouldn't leave her alone," Giselle said, looking back at Karen. Giselle hoped they would have enough care in their heart to allow the abandoned girl to tag along. "Fine, let her come. But, you're responsible for her," Karen said sternly as she walked away annoyed.

The three women and little girl snuck out of the dining room past Silver's guards. They made their way into the hallway towards a large luxurious winding staircase. "Where do we go from here?" Elizabeth asked. "I don't know," Karen replied. "I know where to go," Maddy said. Karen and Elizabeth glanced at Giselle, wondering if they should trust the little girl's judgment. "She has lived here her entire life. She has to know more than us," Giselle said secretly unsure if she was making the right call.

They all followed Maddy up the staircase, down the hall, and to the elevator. She hit the elevator button, taking them to the fifth floor of the house. The woman all stepped off the elevator in unison. They walked down a long hallway that was covered in abstract works of art. "Are you sure we're going the right way?" Giselle asked. "I'm sure," Maddy replied as she skipped down the hallway excited to lead the girls on an adventure.

Maddy stopped skipping, and turned around to face the women who were talking amongst themselves. "Shhh," she said. "There is a guard around the corner. He is guarding the door you will need to go in." "How are we going to get inside with a guard standing in front of the door?" whispered Elizabeth. "I have a plan," said Maddy. "I'll create a distraction and you all can sneak into room 555 when the coast is clear." "No," Giselle said, we can't let you do that. "Too late," Maddy said as she ran off skipping around the corner.

Maddy skipped down the hall, bumping into the guard and falling to the floor pretending to break out into a loud cry. The guard kneeled down to help her as she cried. She explained to the guard that she was lost and was only trying to find her way back to the nursery. The guard helped her up from the floor and assisted her back to the nursery. Maddy had bought them just enough time to sneak into the room and find Jonathan.

The woman charged their way towards the door. They opened the door shocked to find Jonathan, kneeling on the floor as Magnus approached him pinning a crest onto his robe. "Dr. Jonathan Meadows, you are now officially a member of the Illuminus Society. You may now rise," Magnus said as he noticed the three women standing in the room.

"What's going on?" Elizabeth blurted out. "We have been looking for you everywhere," she said as she reshaped her tone to a less questionable one. "There's food and drink in the dining hall and we wanted you to join us," Karen added. They wanted to appear as inconspicuous as possible. "I apologize for keeping you from your friends," Magnus replied. "You can run along and join the others and share the good news with everyone," he said. "Of course, I will sir. And,thanks again for having me," Jonathan said kindly as he led the women away with him back into the hallway.

"What are you doing here?" Elizabeth whispered as they made their way to the elevator. "Are you trying to get yourself killed?" "No," Jonathan replied. "However, I am trying to get answers and protect you in the process." "I don't need you to protect me, Jonathan. I am grown. Besides, I don't think you're any match against guards with guns and ghosts with no head," Elizabeth exclaimed.

"I've been doing some digging. I found a lot of questionable information about Illuminus," Jonathan said. "Apparently, there are a lot of members who are not happy with the leadership of the Queen Mother. There have been a lot of unhappy campers since the founding member Sam Brown died. I overheard some members talking about how they feel she is more concerned with power than change. There has also been talk that Queen Mother had a secret legacy of children that Sam fathered. The other members believe that the Queen Mother found a way to harvest Sam's sperm and have created multiple children she hopes will continue the legacy of Illuminus when she is long gone. The induction ceremony is rumored to be the Queen Mother's induction ceremony for the children she left behind."

"I was brought in by the guards, and I managed to talk them into inducting me in. I appeared to be an Illuminus fanatic to them by expressing my dire need to change the culture of black excellence. I offered my assistance as the first on-site, Doctor of Psychology that they have ever had here," Jonathan concluded. "Welcome to black history," Karen said sarcastically as she listened to Jonathan hash out his plan aloud.

"The ghost you all saw tonight was my former client Omari Bronson. I don't know how he was here or why. But, I plan to find out. I'm also going to find out what this Illuminus Society is all about, and bring them down if they are hurting people," he concluded. He went on to express his plan, "But, I can't do that alone. So, I would need help". He looked at the three women waiting for volunteers. "I'm in," said Elizabeth, then Karen. Giselle stood in front of the elevator silent and deep in thought. "Giselle, Giselle," Elizabeth called out. "What about you? Are you with us or not?" "I don't know," she responded.

"This is all happening so fast, and none of it is making any sense to me."

Elizabeth pulled her to the side. "I know we just met and there's no way for you to feel comfortable placing your trust in the hands of a complete stranger. However, we are all in the same boat here. We've all been invited to be a part of something clueless to what that something actually consists of. Judging from the accusations the messy ghost was throwing around, you may be in search of more answers than all of the rest of us," Elizabeth said. "I saw that little girl, and looking at her, I'd have to say that at first glance she definitely looks like she could be your little sister or your daughter. That has to be worth further investigating.

There was something about Elizabeth's way that reminded Giselle of her cousin Tamra. She hated questioning her past, especially when trying to make sense of the present. But, she knew Elizabeth had a point. They all were in the same boat. If they were going to find the answers they desired, they were going to have to do so as a team. Giselle agreed to join them on their quest for answers. They entered the elevator and watched the doors close as they made their way back to the dining hall to join the other inductees.

Today had been full of surprises, but they all knew tomorrow would bring more. A few hours in the Illuminus mansion, and the veil of mystery had already been partially lifted. Omari's spirit had shaken up the entire commencement process, leading everyone on a mission to find the answers to the questions that were compiled in their minds by the minute. The group of newbies didn't know what was going to happen, but they knew they would not stop until they found the answers, they deserved and desired.

To be continued……………..

ZYIA CONSULTING
Illuminate & Transcend

www.ingramcontent.com/pod-product-compliance
Lightning Source LLC
Chambersburg PA
CBHW060353310726
48976CB00003B/810